FLOWERS

of

BAGHDAD

BRUCE LYMAN

FOURTH ESTATE

Fourth Estate
An imprint of HarperCollins*Publishers*
First published in Australia in 2012
by HarperCollins*Publishers* Australia Pty Limited
ABN 36 009 913 517
harpercollins.com.au

HarperCollins*Publishers*
Level 13, 201 Elizabeth Street, Sydney NSW 2000, Australia
31 View Road, Glenfield, Auckland 0627, New Zealand
A 53, Sector 57, Noida, UP, India
77–85 Fulham Palace Road, London W6 8JB, United Kingdom
2 Bloor Street East, 20th floor, Toronto, Ontario M4W 1A8, Canada
10 East 53rd Street, New York NY 10022, USA

National Library of Australia Cataloguing-in-Publication entry:

Lyman, Bruce.
  Flowers of Baghdad / Bruce Lyman.
  978 0 7322 9505 9 (pbk.)
A823.4

Cover design and photography by Darren Holt, HarperCollins Design Studio
Background cover images by shutterstock.com
Author photograph by Glenyss Barnham
Typeset in Goudy Old Style Regular by Kirby Jones

Bruce Lyman worked on a dairy farm when he left school, then spent many years in government, retiring from that work as an intelligence officer. He was a co-founder of a technology company, which he led to a listing on the stock exchange, before leaving the commercial world to work for an aid agency. Bruce enjoys travel (the remoter the better), bushwalking, murdering a guitar, mentoring teens and young adults, creative writing (www.fast-twitch.blogspot.com) and blogging (see his blog: www.pickledeel.com). He has four adult children and lives in Sydney.

1

Malik

My neighbour was putting out the rubbish when he was shot in the back of the head. The bullet ripped open the left side of Ismail's face, shattering his molars and blasting some of his face onto the street. A piece of jaw bone and a small patch of bloody mud were the only mortal clues he had ever existed. The only other signs that suggested that a man who looked like him and went by his name was ever made by God and lived on His earth were the rigidly posed photos in his house. But then, as sometimes happens in this precious country of mine – this fountain of all human civilisation and source of mankind's wisdom and purity and cleverness – a torso that might have been Ismail surfaced months later. It was difficult to identify the body, and no one wanted to let go of the possibility that maybe a laughing Ismail would walk back down our road, tell a joke to the street vendors and the guards, and then go inside to his wife.

We have too much hard-won hope to let that vision slip away so easily.

Ismail had taken one bag of rubbish to the street and was fetching the second on a calm, warm spring evening, which hinted at the heat and dust to come. The tall gate that hid his house was open, and his youngest son watched through the gap as a man walked up behind his father and executed Ismail at point-blank range. The child has not spoken since but wakes in his sleep screaming for his baba. Neighbours reported that a dusty white van drove off with Ismail's body. There was no word for many weeks, but when a body was finally excavated from a pit, along with other desiccated corpses, its head was missing and the feet and hands had been hacked off. Roughly, as if with an axe. The only clues for his family were the clothes this body wore. They were the same as those Ismail had dressed in that day. But they were the same as so many others too. Maybe it was Ismail. Maybe it was not. Some time afterwards, a mummified head was found buried with a collection of others, also in the hot sand outside the city. Sadly for his family this head was recognisably Ismail and they had to accept he was gone.

There was no reason for him to be killed. He was not a member of a sect, or political group. He was a junior clerk working for the Ministry of Public Works. I have no idea why he was shot. Maybe just for being in the wrong place at the wrong time. Maybe to intimidate everyone else in the neighbourhood. Just shot for taking out his rubbish. A warning to the rest of us perhaps.

I am very careful when I am out on the street. If I glance in the right direction, I can see the black stain of Ismail's blood on the road imprinted with the pattern of tyres that drove through his sticky remains a few short hours later. If I need a reminder to take care when I go to work, Ismail's warning screams off the bitumen every single day.

My name is Malik and I live in Baghdad. I leave my house opposite Ismail's in the suburbs each day and drive to work. And now I am extra cautious when I take out the rubbish. I am always wary each time I step onto our street. You might think we do not walk out on the street. But we have to live. There are five million of us here, trying to live as we always have. There should be more but many have fled. Maybe there are only four million. I do not know. How many are five million souls? Maybe two million more than Berlin? Or maybe two million more than Singapore. I would like to visit there one day. I hear it is a very safe city.

We are a whole community, not just a series of explosions on the evening news. We go to school. We shop. We still drive to and from work. And we continue to put out our rubbish, take our children to the local park and walk towards the river and back. We do not walk along the river bank yet, for there you are exposed and can be shot at from a long distance. Vehicles drive quickly along the river bank, varying their speed to throw off the aim of the snipers who play their sport at our expense. But apart from not going near the Tigris, we still try and live on our streets. Even if our mummified skulls, parchment-black skin pulled back off our mouths, and unkempt hair full of sand, are foraged out of desert pits by curious and hungry dogs. We must live. I must live. I need to believe that one day I will die in peace and be buried with my fathers in honour, not discarded like a cheap plastic bag in the Tigris. I live every day in that hope.

There are palms and olive trees and a small patch of grass outside my house. The house has high walls around it like many houses in this country. The wall is a mud brown but the deep purple of a bougainvillea makes it look bright. I worry about that flower. It may draw attention to my family. But I do not have the heart to destroy it. I have grown up behind walls all my life. It is hard to get out of the habit of trusting those walls. In these hot and hazy days, with the air full of the sounds of war, it is not good to drop my guard. I am careful to look up and down the street as I leave the house each morning. I look to see everything is routine, but it is hard to work out what is normal. If there are some dogs, the sound of birds and the sound of traffic on the highway half a block away I feel a little safe. Sometimes there is a silence in the streets which I cannot explain. On those days I stay at home and hope no one tries to steal from my shop.

I drive an old Datsun with dented panels. It has three bullet holes in the front passenger door and shrapnel gashes on the trunk. The windscreen is damaged from a rock and it runs on retread tyres. I know, I know, they are not safe. I had not seen retreads here when Saddam was in charge, but these days getting parts for cars is hard and I have to use what I can. The steering wobbles too.

I drive through streets of tanks and guns and soldiers and get nervous when I approach a barricade. They are temporary-looking things, very different from the major checkpoints set up at important sites around the city. These are not as well organised and choke up the local traffic in all directions. Anything can happen here. Fear swirls and sniffs around these places. I can taste and smell it, as I do today. I am held up at one roadblock. Out of nowhere a convoy of armoured SUVs, maybe carrying a VIP, cuts through the traffic. An American soldier indicates what he wants me to do by putting his rifle into his shoulder, leaning forward and jerking the muzzle at me. I back up. There are cars packed all around and behind me. I can go no further. I hope he does not shoot. People in cars beside me get out and put their hands up. Just in case. They take no chances with this American. He is a young man. Young men with guns are more dangerous than old men with guns. I don't see many old men with guns.

The convoy passes and we are allowed to creep forward. I do not look at the American in his body armour and wraparound sunglasses. He scans beyond me at the new cars approaching. I drive past Iraqi police and their Hummers. Some of the bigger vehicles have large guns mounted on them, weaponry I recognise from my time in the army. Russian twin 23-millimetre cannon –

designed to shoot down aircraft – being used for traffic control? Allah, be merciful; if they hit my car with those guns, retreads will be the least of my worries.

Around the roadblocks there are police with many types of machine guns and armoured cars constructed with old steel plate. They park on the side of the road and direct their weapons up and down the street. What are they aimed at? What are they protecting? I have no idea. I drive past a locked-down Bradley armoured personnel carrier. It looks dormant and sleepy, but who knows who is in there and what they are watching?

I get past all the roadblocks and the traffic speeds up. Not enough to alarm the security people but enough to relieve me. I do not like these young men and their guns. They can be too eager to use them. Things explode here for no reason. I see another fleet of SUVs take no chances and block the traffic so the car they are protecting can race through. It is efficient. But the average Iraqi living here is not as safe as these VIPs. The average Iraqi just dies if something goes bang.

I was in the army once but now I sell shirts on the edge of the traffic circle. I cannot afford to replace the glass in the windows and have to rely on a steel grille to keep the shop secure at night. Shops on either side of mine are locked in the same way. No one parks in front of my store, and few walkers want to stop, just in case they become random targets of violence. No one lingers here anymore. For their safety people prefer to drive; a moving target is harder to hit. That is how they feel, although cars are bombed too. Perhaps they think they are doing something to protect themselves, and that if they die they can say to Allah, 'I did not die idle.' So no one is idle in front of my shop. Any pedestrians are in a hurry to go somewhere else. Stopping can be fatal.

The shirts are stacked in their plastic boxes, straight and in line with each other. I like these stacks to be neat. At the beginning of each day I wipe the sand and dust off the plastic. Since the glass has been broken I do not turn on the air-conditioner. I could not pay for the electricity if I did. I sweep the footpath and clean off the sand and dust blown in overnight by the oven-hot winds. Every vehicle could carry a bomb, but I try to ignore the cars turning through the traffic circle so close to me and greet Mahrus, who owns the shop next door. He is an old man, thin and leathery with a darkly etched face, his dancing black eyes watery bright, set deep in their sockets. The darkness of his complexion is highlighted by a full beard which frames his face, but without a moustache connecting each side. He prefers to wear an old white cloak after the fashion of the Bedouin, from whom he is descended. He proudly wears the *kufiya* cloth and the *agal* rope, which helps keep it in place on his head. He is respected around these shops for his honesty and directness.

I like Mahrus because he ignores my disfigured face. Where hair should grow there is only smooth skin on the side of my head. It was burned a long time ago in Iran. Some of my face was melted and torn but I thank Allah my eyes were not destroyed, even though an eyelid does not want to stay up during the day. I keep the rest of my hair trimmed short and sometimes people do not see the scar. My beard I am very proud of. My imam calls it a 'Moses beard', it's so thick and full. It is starting to show, some silver and sometimes even orange. Where does that colour come from? Maybe the beard distracts people from seeing my burns. I hope that is the true story, for I am a tall and broad-shouldered man too, and my wife thinks some are afraid of my strength. I pray she is wrong, for I never want to hurt anyone or make them afraid.

Mahrus accepts me as I am, no doubt reflecting his years of accumulated experience and wisdom. Younger men can be less accepting but Mahrus has learned to test and probe a little before making up his mind. He has the air of a compassionate old adviser and I wonder if he was once a tribal counsellor or ambassador. He doesn't say. He carries himself as a man of knowledge and authority, but none in the street press or pry.

We know Mahrus lost his family in Saddam's time, and like most Iraqis he has lost even more loved ones in the last three years. They say there is no family untouched by the recent madness. It's criminal madness. We all know that but we do not say it. Those who do are not in the markets the next morning. We are Sunni and Shia, married in the same house for many, many years. Lots of Iraqis live together like that.

Old Mahrus comes down here every day, stands in his doorway and watches the world turn on the traffic circle in front of him. I say hello and he smiles at me from under his white beard and headgear. His name means 'protected by God'. Maybe that is why he keeps smiling. The rain falls and the sun shines and Mahrus smiles. Yet when bad things happen he still smiles. His eldest boy, his most precious inheritance, is dust in the trenches of Iran. Still he smiles. His sister's family vanishes in the night before the Americans come in 2003. Still he smiles. There are no customers in his shop. Yet he smiles. Protected by God.

I wish we could fix up our shop fronts. The rendering has been blasted off and the bricks look shabby. One day perhaps. At least nothing has exploded here for six months. Maybe this period of quiet will last. They are talking about ending the curfew. That will help. Or will it? So many people have died for no reason except that they were in the wrong place at the wrong time. Like poor Ismail. Shot in the head and his body thrown away. Put the rubbish out and die. For no reason. '*No reason!*' I want to scream. Die for a cause, yes! But these deaths are for no reason, like our war with Iran. No reason. You are mistaken if you think our fights are over religion. This is the work of criminals.

Later, as I drive home, I am careful approaching the roadblock again. I move over to let an American tank go past. If I stop without being directed they might think I have a bomb. I keep rolling at five kilometres per hour, hoping the tank will not crunch me into the concrete wall on the side of the road. I try not to look nervous.

I'm familiar to the soldier on this corner and he clears me through with a nod. The Americans drive past and look elsewhere. I continue on and start to relax just a little bit. I pull up to my house and, as always, I look up and down the street, see nothing to frighten me so get out and open the gate before driving in and locking it behind me. No one bought any shirts today. Maybe tomorrow I will make a sale.

I have three children. One boy and two girls. Mostly they are good but many times they drive me even more crazy than I am now. I am glad I have these children, since they give me hope. I do not tell my wife these things but sometimes I think it would be nice to have more sons. Please, do not think I do not love my daughters, but I once had many brothers and we had a joyous time together. My son needs other boys around him, but there are not many boys his age in our neighbourhood. When I was a boy I would play many kilometres from my home with my brothers, and even as we got older there were many things we would do with our friends away from home. But I am frightened to let my children away from the house. When Imaad walks to and from school that is a terror for me.

I am sorry, I forget my manners. My boy is called Imaad. It can mean a few things and when we named him we were thinking of the support he would provide us through this trouble, which started in 1991 when so many families were broken and flung about. My girls are Aalia and Fatimah. Both are good fun, always giggling and playful, with dark eyes that sparkle with mischief.

You know, Fatimah was named after my wife's niece. Such a good girl and very pretty.

Many times I am sad for the family, but especially my children. Not because of the future. I have to believe the future will be good for them. But because of the past. They have no past. They have no childhood. Oh, they play like children. But it is careful play. They do not run up the street to play with their friends. They do not go down to the river to play with boats. They do not play in the park on the corner unless we are with them. What they live is normal. But they could be more normal. More safe. More carefree. I wish so much they could be safer and more carefree.

The traffic has been clogged worse than usual and I am late. I greet Imaad and kiss my wife and go to look in on the girls. It is a hot September evening and they are sprawled across their beds, uncovered and uncaring. This is the time I look at them and understand only in their sleep are they carefree and childlike. It is sad they do not know it.

Ah, I forget myself. Here I am talking about my family and I have not introduced my wife. Her name is Saleema. She is a very still person. No, maybe that is perhaps not the right word. She is a very calm person so she is good for me. Maybe that is why she was such a good nurse. I worry too easily, but it takes much to ripple Saleema's still pond. She did get anxious about a grey hair she found recently. How women concern themselves about such things!

The story of how we met is an unusual one. I will tell you one day. When I was a younger man I was embarrassed to tell it, but Saleema and her family and her friends always thought it was funny. Eventually I relented and could see what they laughed at. Nowadays I think it is an amusing tale compared to the stories of murder that happen in this city.

A half-moon hangs in the sky. I'm sitting on my flat roof, leaning back on a dusty poolside recliner. Ha-ha, no, there is no pool. I sit in a lightly stirring hot breeze, listening and watching. It is tranquil but not quiet. This city is such a strange and seething and unquiet place when the sun is up, but it mutters in its sleep and tosses and turns with bad dreams. It is early and my city is only starting to stir in its sleep on this hot night. It is a softer city in the dusky light than the one I see during the day. Frogs among the eucalypts pulse their quiet songs in a soothing rhythm. They sound to me like a blues band. Distant mosques broadcast their calls and prayers in a melodic tone that is beguiling, a soft chorus that hints at more civil and ordered things. Of better things. The thoughts and dreams of a more civil city raise my spirits. I like to think about a civilised Baghdad, and up here on these nights I am sure I can feel it as well as hear it. Such prospects can make a man happy.

The rumble of traffic lends its background hum. Flares drift down through the trees. Silent, and betraying an unheard and unseen helicopter. Sometimes the drone of engines buzzing on surveillance, also unseen, can be heard drifting in and out of the peaceful stillness, which is also broken now and then by Pumas or Blackhawks thundering in pairs over the house, roaring in then fading out in seconds. Leaving me again to the mullahs and the frogs. A civil airliner flashes its strobes as it traces its line north, unlike the invisible military jets that bore through the sky, in and out much more quickly. It is in this quietness that I hope for my children, for my family, for Mahrus, for this city. Under this velvet I can imagine us normal and quiet again. Somehow my horror of the hurt lashed into each other fades away on my rooftop, and especially tonight as I sit up here under the moonlight and soak up the evening. The frogs are now the constant background theme, far better than the murderous noises I have heard during the day, when dull booms told me someone had died an indiscriminate and senseless death. My rooftop is my shrine to the peace that has to come. Just don't tell my imam. He will want to know why I am not in the mosque at prayer. Up on this rooftop I find peace. This is my true place of prayer and worship.

2

Aadil

Thank you for visiting me in this American gulag. You can see from the tag tied to my wrist that my name is Aadil. It is not a good way to be introduced. But you see it before I can say it. What can I do? My wife is not able to visit me here in this cell. I would not want her to see me like this even if she could. Ha, I am not even sure if she knows I am here. I have not been able to speak with anyone other than prisoners for a week. I scarcely believe I have been here a week. I thought I would be dead by now. The men they arrested with me are here too. We try not to talk to each other. You do not know who is listening. The police are the police. They do not beat us like they might have in the old days. Not as much. You look like you do not believe me. Look here at these bruises and poorly bandaged gashes. I got these injuries when I was arrested.

You want to hear my story? I am not so sure telling you my story is a safe thing to do. Who are you working for, really? I do wonder that. I look at you and your reserved demeanour. You are not frightened of being down here. That tells me you are very ignorant or you are protected by someone I should fear. You have more protection than just your press pass might give you. And if you are ignorant, well, let's just say that while we might be in a secure facility at the moment I have no idea where your dictaphone might end up. You might be careful with it and yet it becomes lost and then who will find it? Will Satan uncover it as he stalks this hell we have conjured up from our cradle? He prowls this land, you know, cloaked in dust and heat and masked by the sighs and cries of our mothers and wives. He may find that recording and hand it over to one of his demons who drives an old, faded BMW and cradles in his lap a Russian assault rifle and kills just for the sheer exultation of it. You understand, do you not, that little machine could kill my family? Could kill me … if we are not dead already.

Ah, I am talking through a hole in my head. Why do you ask me about my English? Your question tells me you are not listening. But I will tell you anyway. Maybe there is salvation in the talking, for something needs to atone for the sins of my actions. I will talk if you will listen – and do some small things for me. You nod? I am amazed how agreeable you are. Do not commit to something until you hear the proposal. You have heard that before, no? Heard but not learned, I think.

You do not want to know me. Not even my neighbours and family will want to know me now. Our conversations will be superficial and distant, as if they sense something poisonous in me. They would be right. And if my mother, bless her soul, knew what I did she would shriek and collapse on the ground in despair. But what was I to do? I have nine children. All good children. Yet since Saddam left, some go to school, some do not. Until I had this work some were not able to eat each day. The young ones always ate first, and on most days of the week. My older children did not complain, even when they went to bed hungry. What was I to do? Let them starve? You shake your head. No, you are right. But how could I do the things I have done? You will judge me with your eyes and your words and your writing when you hear what I have to say.

But what is that to you? You who have come in from Jordan, spiralling down in a safe Airbus flown by South Africans, not those tired-looking aircraft flown by Iraqi Airways. Yes, yes, I know that flight too. All those precautions against a missile threat that might exist. Or might not. See, you do not know us. How can you know us? But you want to see. You are curious and came here to understand the darkness in our souls, for here darkness spills out of the human heart, unrestrained and in all its glory.

No? Come now, of course that is why you have sought me out. I assume that is why you endured the long bureaucratic wait to get permission to speak to a prisoner. You want to talk and you want to understand. That is something. But you should be prepared to taste the bitterness of the human heart. For here in this ancient place demons claw their way to the surface while angels fall from the sky to tumble together in the sand and fire of this land. You will taste the evil of worm-ridden, rotten human hearts, yet stand under the sweet, cleansing water of the fountain of human kindness. Here is where you find God's pinnacle creature at his best and at his worst.

I do not want to talk, but maybe this story can ease my judgment in another life. Are you ready for me, you on the free side of the bars? Are you ready for my story? Are you ready for foulness and sweetness together in your mouth? It is a story you will not be able to rinse out for a long time. Yet it is not very much different from thousands of other stories in this country. Except that for the moment I still live. Turn off the recorder. I will tell my story. Turn it off and leave it on the table where I can see it turned off. I do not want you to turn it on in your pocket. See what Iraq has made me? You are not a threat to me but I do not trust you. I am a Cain, not an Abel.

Let me start how we should properly have started. My name is Aadil. I was a colonel in the Republican Guard. My work in the army was electrical engineering. I am a good engineer and can get power running in most places it is needed. I specialised as a young officer on electrical circuits in vehicles. Later I expanded my knowledge to power grids and I spent two years working for the Ministry of Electricity, learning how power was delivered across the country. It is wondrous to see high-voltage power make its way to a small village where everyday people can use it. I liked doing that sort of work, making life better for ordinary people, that is. Then I went back to the army and concentrated on making sure military units on the move had all the power they needed. A headquarters needs lots of electricity to watch all that sport on television … you are allowed to smile down in these cells, you know.

Only an army engineer, I see you thinking. Not something more exotic like the special forces fighting at night. You are right. Ordinary work, though I can see from your face you wonder how I got here. Shaking your head will not convince me. Let's keep going. Whether you wish to listen or not I care nothing. I am going to talk and hopefully God can see the repentance in my heart a little better if He hears it from my lips too. Do you believe in God? I thought not. In Iraq you have to believe in God. No, not because we are slaves to a religion. But because we have to hope that there is some good somewhere in this universe.

You smile but I tell you, goodness does not exist here. It can if we let it but, given what I have seen, I know in my heart there is no possibility for good. I am here as a prisoner, about to die at the hand of someone I know not, because there is no good in the heart of this place. The English have a saying, you know. They talk about a heart of darkness. If there is a black heart of this earth it beats in this place. From your face I see you think I am a cynical, dried-out old Guard. Maybe I am, maybe I am. Maybe the tears of repentance will soften me a little and God will judge me less harshly for that when I see Him.

When I was a junior officer the army asked me to join the Ba'ath Party. It was a friendly interview but it was not friendly at the same time, if you know what I mean. It was like meeting the father of your future wife. Friendly on the surface but hostile underneath. If I said no to the invitation I would never get promoted or be allowed to study overseas and my family would never have access to scholarships, new cars and other benefits. So I said yes and the meeting stayed friendly. The Ba'ath Party was a good party to belong to. It gave me privileges, and when I was a junior officer I was not expected to attend any meetings or rallies. Just being a member was enough to show I was a true Iraqi, and to be trusted. I was happy to be left alone and to get my training done.

In 2003 my country fell apart. You know that story. Even though the country was in disarray I hoped there would be lasting peace in the end. The Americans moved too quickly for us, but I think that was a good thing. The vehicles in my unit were not destroyed and I was pleased so few men died. None from my unit were killed. We all watched the Americans in their rapid sweep along the Tigris and into the city. It was fast. We debated what to do and decided we would be safe if we stayed away from them. So we did. The days after the battle for Baghdad were strange. About a week after the statues were torn down, cautious American soldiers visited our barracks. They were nervous but polite. We showed them our armoury and they took away our weapons. We were allowed to keep our pistols. We did not show them the buried weapons stashed for years and years, should the armies of satanic Iran ever reach this far. Or the other weapons buried as part of Fedayeen preparations to counter any uprising against Saddam. We did not think those caches would be of any importance to the American situation. The American soldiers would be gone soon and we would be allowed to run our country anew with Saddam out of the way.

I was very surprised the Americans did not want me in the army. I lost my job overnight and was told to leave the barracks. Even now I am feeling angry and humiliated when I speak of it. I am a professional engineer with years of education in Germany. I also have excellent English from my studies and all my time overseas. The military paid for my language studies. The Americans could have used me to help rebuild. It would have given me pride to do these things. But I am a member of the Ba'ath Party, see? And the American bureaucrats thought that made me a follower of Saddam and maybe even a great Satan too. I argued and pleaded but the young man in a suit and tie from the State Department run by our new dictator Bremer would not look me in the eye. He just said I had no part to play in the new Iraq. People like me were not wanted. I was condemned as a criminal.

So I had no pay. No money to feed my children. There is no social security as there is in your country. And no pension if you lose your employment. There was no school for the children now, and there was no power. Our small freezer no longer worked. Vegetables would store, but we had no food to put in the freezer anyway. The infrastructure that helped supply our food was gone and I could not access my bank account. So many days were spent waiting for banks that never opened. The television would not work. My children searched around the suburbs and one of my sons got a job running messages for the Americans. His money allowed us to eat rice once a day.

To keep busy I rebuilt an old military generator my neighbours helped me steal one night. We pulled it into the lane between our houses. One man found some hangar floor paint near the airport where the Americans were rebuilding, and we painted the generator a bright enamel grey, which was better than its old military camouflage. That generator still runs and keeps thirteen houses powered for free. It is free because we still steal the fuel from the Americans to run it. It gave us the television and we were able to tune into Al Jazeera, as well as all those music shows from Lebanon my children love so much. Having that television allowed us to get a view of what was happening across our country. Most importantly, it made us feel connected again. We were not left sitting in the dark. It was a little thing that made us feel civilised.

Efraim was killed by the Americans in an accident. My first born, my precious first-born son. Do you know what I mean? Do you have children? You do? Good, you know, then, what a transformation comes about when the first child is born to you. Whatever happens after that event, nothing can ever be the same. He was the first in our larger family, before all my brothers and sisters had children, so was precious to the extended family too. But he was precious because he was mine. I know it was an accident. In my heart I know it was. He should not have been throwing rocks. And the American soldier was young and nervous. At his funeral I raged and raged. My blessed wife was more composed. Her quiet pain is not my liquid heat. She suffers too, but is busy with our other children.

In the crying and shouting and all the noise and turmoil at the funeral someone pressed a crushed cigarette packet into my hand. I did not see the front of him. Just his back. It was a torn Winston packet, picked up from the ground. I could not tell where it had come from. But the cell number on the slip of paper inside was clear. So too the offer of one hundred United States dollars. That was more money than I had seen in three months and I was surely desperate.

I rang the number a week after my son was buried. No one answered and the number rang out. I tried again the next day. The number was disconnected. So I went out to look for work. American soldiers were trying to fix the local power substation. They did not want my help even though I did not tell them I was in the Ba'ath Party. I think they were put off by my poor clothes and that made me ashamed as well as frustrated.

The next morning I rose early, which is my usual habit. On the front step was a Winston packet with fourteen cigarettes, one hundred United States dollars and a note telling me to wait. I did not know how much time I had to wait, so I used that gift sparingly. I took the foreign notes to a man I know down at the river. It was a long walk that day but I returned with fresh vegetables, a bag of apples, more dates than we had seen since I was sacked, black-market dinars, and some of that flavoured herbal tea my wife likes so much. I bought pastries and chocolates. Not too many, just enough to put a smile on the face of all those children. Each one is special. Each child is another unplumbed measure of love from which I draw. It matters not that we have so many. Even this old officer has a soft spot for each one.

The pastries were placed on a large porcelain plate and set on the table. There was silence for a moment then a clamour of delight. None reached forward but each looked at me, a sea of tantalised eyes and tousled hair and bursting amazement.

'These are ours?'

I nodded. Glances were stolen at the tray.

'Really ours?'

'Indeed, they are,' I confirmed. 'I have had some good fortune and hope now things have turned.' They acknowledged my words, but truly their ears did not hear. They had eyes only for the plate before them. 'Okay, after your mother has chosen her pastry you can help yourselves.' That night the family talked and joked as carefree as I had heard them in many months.

* * *

It was three weeks before I met Halim, a dark-eyed, brooding man. In the beginning I believed he had a good heart, a prophet's heart. My impression was that he was not for this world but for the betterment of the rest of us. Pure and undefiled. Yet hard and unyielding. I look back on that now and see how deluded I was for he proved no prophet. He is dead or in this prison maybe. If he is down here in one of these neighbouring cells and can overhear me, he will no doubt laugh at how eager I was to believe him. But I needed an honourable way to provide for my family and it was through those eyes that I viewed this man. I was desperate but that did not calm my unease about the first meeting.

When you live in this place you trust only your family. And even then I have to tell you there are sad stories of brothers betraying brothers. And outside your family you might just trust school friends or neighbours. But those you know well are still people you are careful with. Here, someone was suggesting a meeting and I did not know what the person looked like let alone understand the substance of his heart or the stillness of his soul. This man might be the man who would kill me. Maybe in the end he has done just that. But I was caught and had to meet him when he demanded. Why? Because I had taken his money and my family had enjoyed the benefits of that gift. I was deep in his debt for such a small amount of cash.

His instructions were simple. We would meet in the early evening at a café, just a few blocks from my house. We would meet before the café got too busy, when most people in the area were distracted by the evening meal and the call to prayer. He did not say all that, of course, but the time was unusual for business. I expected something later at night.

After the date, time and place arrived in three separate Winstons over the course of a week I wandered down to the café to look around. I wasn't really sure what I was searching for. Was there something special about this place that appealed to him? Was he watching me? I think he must have been. The café was quiet, but as the evening drew darker, more men gathered to talk and to watch football on the small television strapped to a shelf high on the wall.

The café was run by Saleh. I knew Saleh from my army days. I knew him not well, but enough to be wary of him, and also to respect him. You wonder that I should be wary? The answer may surprise you. You see, Saleh once worked in the security directorate responsible for testing the loyalty of those of us in senior positions. It was not unusual for men of my rank to be reviewed by the security service, and we had always to be on our guard. On those occasions we met, Saleh would declare his agenda and interview me very directly. I imagine his reports would have gone back to the sons of Tikrit and been compared with any clandestine assessments from sources hidden among our ranks.

I had been in Saleh's café many times and we had talked of football and families and in some way you might even say we were friends; but we never mentioned the past. You think I was paranoid, eh? With men like Saleh you always wonder. Are they still in government service? Do they still have connections? Maybe his café is a front and not the family business he pretends. He is a decent man. He was good at his job – good at drawing out information. There were men like him who could apply subtle pressure and not resort to violence. Yet that is not enough to ensure he is not picked up by the Americans. Have they not yet found his records in all those government files they freighted out of this city in 2003? He is a lucky man. Or he works still for some unseen directorate. For now I simply count him as lucky. But, for all that, I do not allow myself to get too close. I am always watchful.

What was I looking for as I greeted Saleh and scouted his café? I do not really know but a meeting in a café run by an ex-security man made me doubly nervous. And when I am nervous I sense things that are not right. Things that are out of place. People who have nothing to do but watch. Those people stand out. People with things to hide. They stand out too. But, you know, despite my caution and worry, there was nothing unusual. There was nothing I could sense that was abnormal. No Americans came this far down the narrow lanes to disturb us. No secret police. No people except those who wanted to argue politics over coffee and shout at each other about football played in Europe.

On the appointed day I dressed carefully and with as much dignity as my tired and worn civilian clothes would allow. I wanted to convey rank and authority as best I could. I arrived early, sat towards the back, and watched the lanes as men wandered up and down and children played and the dust swirled and the heat baked the buildings. Halim quietly stepped in right on time, gazed around the café, lifted his chin to Saleh, who started to prepare his coffee, then moved over to the table, selecting a chair beside me rather than opposite. He wanted to watch the door and the front just as much as I did. He seemed placid yet in control, above the noise and strife outside, a balm for my screaming heart and fractured soul. I think that man knew how ready I was to get to work, and to ask no questions.

He moved quickly into a briefing about what he needed. He had some design work for me, he said. Could I build electrical circuits with relays for him? Clever circuits that could not be tampered with, or interfered with by stray or even targeted signals? Circuits that would respond to his instructions only?

Ha, I see you are interested now. How has the ordinary army engineer become special now?

'Who is Halim?' you ask. You will see, you will see. Get me some news about my wife and I will tell you more. For now, just listen.

Halim cautioned me to ask no questions if I wanted to be paid. I would receive five hundred United States dollars per week for a month. He would double that amount if my circuits were reliable. I told him I needed parts, boards, etching material, tools and solder.

It was a conversation full of promise and threat all at once. A dying man reaches for what he can. I reached for the promise and grasped its welcoming softness. But underneath there was the hardness of death. I guess I will feel its full effect soon enough when they carry out their prison justice on me.

Even as I grasped the promise I was worried about why they had selected me. What had I done to stand out and be noticed by these people? Who was I to them? Halim was expecting my questions.

'We only work with people who are recommended to us. You are a senior officer and you have a number of supporters who commended you to us, but not just because you are a senior officer.'

'But that is not why you want me?'

'Your seniority? Oh yes, it is certainly something we like. You never know when we might need someone with your rank to speak with other senior people.'

'Retired rank.'

'Come now, you know you never leave those ranks behind.'

I nodded. He was right.

'But you don't want me just for my seniority. There are so many men out there in the same position I am in.'

'True. The recommendation was based on your engineering skills. We know you were a talented electronics designer as a younger man and everyone speaks well of your work. We would simply like you to do that work again.'

'So why approach me the way you did?'

'Look, we know you are in a difficult situation. We had a recommendation. We can help you and you can help us. That's it. Okay?'

Halim was becoming irritated and I knew I had to back off. I would test him some more as I got to know him better. But there at the end was the real reason. They knew I was desperate and unlikely to decline their offer. How I hated that I could do nothing but accept.

Before the meeting drew to a close I asked Halim to repeat his instructions. I needed to ensure I understood them clearly. With men like Halim their suspicion can kill you. Get a brief wrong and they might assume you are trying to thwart them. How do you Americans say it? Shoot and ask questions later? Yes, that is what Halim would do if somehow I misunderstood him. Shoot me and find someone else.

'I am to design and build some electrical switching equipment. That is the task I am asked to do?'

Halim nodded but I had to press him further. I knew it would be complicated. I reminded him I needed to act with care so if the Americans searched me or my house they would not suspect anything untoward.

Halim did not react and stared back at me. It was a blank look and I wondered if he had understood. His dark eyes and prophet's mind now chilled me. I started to feel this was already lethal. Then he softened a little. 'You should not even take that risk.'

'The risk of making these?'

'No, the risk of ever being caught making them.'

'You are thinking they are dangerous.'

'Do you want me to spell out what these devices are for?'

'No, no, I already know. Let us leave it at that. If no one has ever said what I am to do I can deny I was ever told.'

Halim nodded and murmured words that tinged the metal of my heart. 'You know, I was in the army with you?'

I told him I knew him from somewhere and that the army may well have been the place. The knowledge left me cold. These men knew where I lived, who I was and what my networks might be. I thought I had escaped the webs but here I was in the middle of one so sticky I could feel its entrapment all over me.

'Do you know what happens if I pull out now?' I asked him.

'Best not think about that – that path takes you somewhere your family will find even more unpleasant than you. Let's think about where you are to build these things.'

He smiled the only full smile I ever saw on his face, handed me a packet of cigarettes and left the café.

In the safety of my house I opened the cigarette box and found one thousand dollars in fifties and an address. I hid the money behind an electricity distribution board in my kitchen and burned the address. Then I went to a man I know in the markets and changed one of the notes. He handed me a small bundle of soiled local money and called me 'sir', the first time I had been acknowledged this way since I was discharged from the army. I bought some pomegranates, dates and raisins and watched my wife and children cheerful again as they ate that night. I felt strong again seeing them like that. Maybe this would work out. When the imams called us to prayer that night under a hot white moon my forehead touched the ground, as it had numerous times before. My heart prayed for hope and peace for my family, and just briefly my hate for the killers of my son was replaced by a joy for life and a hope for old age for the rest of my children. I prayed again before I lay down to sleep …

> *Our Lord! Take us not to task*
> *   if we forget, or make a mistake.*
> *Our Lord! Charge us not with a load such as You laid*
> *   on those before us.*
> *Our Lord! Do not burden us beyond what we have*
> *   strength to bear.*
> *And pardon us and forgive us, and have mercy on us.*
> *You are our protector.*
> *And help us against the people of the unbelievers.*

3

Malik

I leave the rooftop and cover the three children with their sheets. I pause and watch them, still and calm with their arms flung open in an innocence which I envy. How lovely their lashes on their angel cheeks and how steady their breathing. No dark demons ever seem to chase their dreams and I love them all the more for that. They stir a little under the adjusted sheets, stretch but do not wake, comfortable in the warm darkness. I go down the cool marble stairs to the centre room in our house where it is so still and hot the children refuse to sleep there. But Saleema, my wife, will sleep nowhere else. She will not lie near an open window. I think if we are to be bombed we are to be bombed. But she needs me, so I lie down on the bed and listen to her sleeping. Soon I sleep too.

I am woken in the morning by the early call to prayer but I leave them alone. I do not go to the mosque at that hour. I hear the squeak of the bicycle wheeled by an elderly neighbour on his way to worship. He told me he did some bad things as a young man and needs to say all the prayers he can. He is a sad man, weighed down with too many cares. Nevertheless, but perhaps because of this, he rides tall through all danger. He cares not for any bombs. He fears no slaughter on the kerbside. His sons were executed by Saddam in one of the uprisings in this country. He is lucky to know that. Many just vanished with no explanation. He blames himself and believes God is judging him. So off he squeaks and fades into the morning. I drift back to sleep but not before I hear Saleema stir and leave the bed. She will start cooking and getting Imaad ready for school. It is still dark outside and the day has yet to become as oven-hot as it was when I lay down.

As I open the gates my children stay in the house until I walk into the street. I look around while I sweep and try to be as calm and ordinary as possible. I always sweep the path in the morning. I sweep and look. And listen. Today everything smells, sounds and looks safe, so I finish the cleaning and kiss my children. Saleema is fussing over Imaad's clothes and worrying about his school books, making sure they are packed into his bright blue school bag. He laughs and wriggles away from her, eager to get started on the day.

When I watch them it is hard to not think of Ismail. Do I let Imaad go? But how can I not? Our only other option is to hold our children prisoner in their own home. He leaves, scampering out the door, through the gate and up the street. I wander out behind him through the gateway to watch. He is joined by two friends – two of them hold hands and settle into a walk. The third thinks he is too old to hold hands but stays close, kicking stones in his worn-out shoes and shouting at his friends who are coming out of their homes across the street. We parents hold our breath all day and hope they are safe. They might go to a school with no glass in the windows but they are with their school mates and forgetting the conflict and being normal. I wish for all to be normal.

I kiss Saleema and start the Datsun in its usual coughing cloud of cold-start oil smoke, then steer it away from the house. Saleema closes the gate behind me and I drive to the end of our street, turn left at the palm trees and small park with rusty play things, then slowly push into the traffic. No one is in a rush here. We are all too careful to rush. We look at each other wondering if the man driving in the next lane is armed with a bomb. Will this car trip be my last? I wish we did not have to look at each other with such suspicion. But it is hard not to think this way of young men in their cars. They can be the source of death. Especially when they are not speeding. Just slowly rolling up to you and vanishing in a flash and a bang. Soon I am driving past the young American at the corner roadblock. He nods and waves me on, still hidden behind his wraparound sunglasses, his rifle half raised at us all. Today there is a tank behind him. Its barrel moves oh so slightly left and then right as we creep past, reminding us it is alive and lethal.

I park in a lane off the traffic circle and walk to my shop. Mahrus is already there, waiting on the pavement outside his small shop with his smile. We nod to each other.

'*Assalamu alaikum.*'

'*Wa alaikum assalaam.*'

I like that we start the day well. I open the steel grille and begin wiping off the dust that has accumulated overnight on the plastic cases. It is a long task but I have all day. Mahrus leans in my doorway and starts our conversation. It is idle talk but I like that it is about the usual and the unusual things we see and hear. In this city we hear the boom of explosions almost every day. Once it was each day. Sometimes we hear the tat-tat-tat of a machine gun. Sometimes the thuck and crack of a mortar.

A stray mortar round hit our house one day. I was not up there in my usual place or I might have been wounded or even killed. I do not think anyone was aiming at us. Someone just fired five rounds in our general direction and one landed on the edge of my house. At first I did not know what it was. There was a loud bang and the lights went out. I checked the switches. Nothing. I looked outside and all the street lights were still on. I could hear the generator. The children were still and silent, frozen in their places, sensing something wrong. I looked out the side gate and saw people pointing at the balustrade that runs around the top of the house. It was scarred and the cement render looked as if giant claws had ripped at it. A piece fell with a clatter even while I was at the gate.

When I got to the rooftop I found pieces of metal from the mortar. Sharp and twisted. Most of the metal had fallen into the yard. But some had been flung across the roof, and the window which lets light into the stairwell had been blown out. Metal fragments had cut the power cable to the house and the cable from the television dish but kind neighbours quickly repaired them. Random weapons fired by former neighbours. Fortunately that day no random death. My boy keeps some metal as a souvenir. I know how inaccurate setting up a mortar can be so I know it is unlikely there will be another one hitting the house. Unless we are unlucky.

I have lots of men's shirts in my store. They are good shirts, made in India from good cotton. Polyester fibres are hard to wear in this heat, though many do. Before the American war, trade was good. There are many businesses and government complexes nearby. Men would buy my shirts on their way to work, or in a lunch break. Most often their wives or mothers would buy them. During the first war, when the Americans attacked from the air, my street was littered with debris, although the shop was not damaged. But the shop is across the river from my home and for many weeks I was unable to get to work with all the damaged bridges drowned in the Tigris. When the Americans came back ten years later and fought in the streets, I lost all the glass in my windows. It is hard to buy glass. It is expensive. I have no money for glass. Mahrus has no money and no glass. But he has a solid steel shutter so he can seal his shop from the dust that blows in from the desert. I have an open steel-mesh grille. I used open mesh so that people wandering past after hours could look in and maybe think, 'I will come here tomorrow and buy a beautiful shirt.' Now when I close the mesh I keep the thieves out but not the dust.

So Mahrus stands and chews dates and waits while I wipe down the plastic boxes. Each box has a folded plain-colour shirt. I tried to introduce stripes and patterns once. It was not successful.

'Some dates, my friend?'

'No, thank you. I will stay until I have finished here and the shop is presentable. Customers may walk in at any time and I don't want the goods to be half buried in sand.'

'Customers, you say? You think you will get many customers, not just one?' I can tell Mahrus is amused even though his face shows no expression.

'Yes, you old doubter. I think we will get many. Maybe not all on the one day but many will come. And even if there is only one today it is worth having the shop ready for that person. Maybe that one person will go and tell others they found a beautiful shop among the ruins of our street and others will come to see.'

'Or stay away from someone who is clearly mad.'

'I keep good company, then, don't I, Mahrus? Very good company.' His eyes crease into a shining smile and he helps himself to more of his dates.

'A woman bought some sweets this morning, Malik. I am a happy man.'

'Just one woman?'

'She was walking. She walked to the store, just to buy these sweets.'

'Really? She was not going anywhere else?' I pause in my dusting.

'She said her mother used to buy sweets from me. She is to throw a party for her children and wants to buy *mammoul* and *baklava*. She even asked for chocolate.'

I join in Mahrus's cheer. 'When was the last time you sold anyone chocolate?'

He lifts his shoulders in a dramatic shrug. 'Only Allah can remember that, my friend. It is so long ago. I told her to come back tomorrow and I would give her fresh chocolate. I think the rats have been feasting on my old stock. Only they could eat the stuff. It is so hard. Hard as ceramic tiles.' He cackles. It is the laugh of a man with a weight coming off his shoulders.

When I finish dusting I stand out in the street. Our shops face the traffic circle and there is nowhere for cars to park near us. You might think that is a blessing. You would be right. But this traffic circle leads onto one of the bridges and all the traffic that needs to cross to the International Zone comes past here. When the Americans came, their tanks whined and hissed and rumbled and spewed fire and puffed smoke as they ground through this traffic circle. One shot from their guns and glass in any direction vanished. I was hiding at the back of the shop hoping the roof would not cave in when three rounds were fired. I was deaf for days and

Mahrus bled from his ears. He has a neighbour, a doctor, who fixed him.

So it is a busy intersection and we see lots of things but we do not see enough people. Now Mahrus has received his first customer in many months. I hope they like his sweets. Some have been on the shelves so long they will not be safe to eat. We stand and watch the cars. We say nothing. No more people come to our shops after the single sweet buyer, but our spirits have been lifted. Anything is possible if people are walking to our stores.

I drive home that night as careful as I ever am, past the roadblocks and the young men. The street feels normal as I park the Datsun. On a hot wind I catch the brief whisper of helicopters on the prowl, then they are gone. When I arrive I am greeted by the children who grasp my fingers in excitement and pull me into the kitchen. Sitting at the table with her shawl loosely draped over her shoulders is my wife's niece Fatimah. She is the second daughter of Saleema's older sister, and about ten years younger than my wife. But they have always been friends even though so many years separate them. It is a sad story because all of Fatimah's family are now dead, but she does not speak about it. How can she when so many people have sad stories? She was only nine when she was pulled from the rubble of her house. Something went wrong. One of those stray bombs that are described as collateral damage. Her parents, her two brothers and a sister, along with many neighbours were collateral. Somehow Fatimah survived.

She lives now with her father's family and they are good to her. But she is close to Saleema. They are like sisters.

So Fatimah spends much time with us. My children love her. She spoils them with gifts and plays games and treats them like they are her own. Indeed, Saleema frets that Fatimah is not married with children of her own, even though we just celebrated her twenty-sixth birthday. She is so good with our children and very attractive too. If our little Fatimah grows up to be half as beautiful as her namesake, I will be a very busy father keeping the boys away from her. I hope we all live long enough for that to become a problem for me.

In the meantime we secretly hope for Fatimah to find a man of honour who will understand the treasure she is and marry her and bring her happiness. But for her part, Fatimah puts her hope on hold until Baghdad is a peaceful place.

The children soon tire of me and return to their endlessly patient cousin, and Saleema to her tasks and companionship. I leave them to the noise and bustle of the kitchen. I like the friendship they have, but most often it overwhelms me. I have other things I am worried about and today Fatimah and her future spouse is not one of them.

From the rooftop I hear the sound of high-pitched turbines and the whirr of tanks racing up a nearby highway, though I cannot see any of them. The Americans. They are always in a hurry. The mosques call us to prayer as a hot sun sets in a copper-blue sky.

Perform the prayer
At the sinking of the sun to the darkening of the night
And the recital of dawn;
Surely the recital of dawn is witnessed.
And as for the night, keep vigil a part of it, as a work
    of supererogation for Thee;
It may be that your Lord will
Raise you up to a laudable station.
And say: 'My Lord,
Lead me in with a just ingoing, and lead me out with a
Just outgoing; grant me
Authority from You, to help me.'
And say:
'The truth has come, and falsehood has vanished away;
Surely falsehood
Is ever certain to vanish.'

4

Aadil

I made the money last a long time. Weeks and weeks. For in my heart I knew Halim wanted me to build electronic parts for bombs. His language was careful when he spoke to me and I tried not to show I saw the care he took. He said nothing that would incriminate him if he was ever questioned by the authorities. And my conversation was careful too. I could deny I was ever told anything about weapons, although Halim's intention was clear enough.

I did not wait for him to contact me again before getting ready. I needed to find a safe place to build the parts he wanted. I walked for days under the pretext of looking for work. There was none to be had, of course. But as I entered each small business to approach the owner, I was appraising his premises to see if they were suitable for what I wanted. Some of the best buildings were the modern ones along main roads, but they were not so secure. The farther away from the main roads

I wandered, the farther I distanced myself from the patrolling Americans. But the premises became less and less suitable. Some days I would walk with friends and they would listen in the background as I asked about employment. Some of my friends tried to dissuade me from the hunt, but most understood I had to inquire even if the result was already known. It is a matter of honour, not results. But they never knew my real intention.

I had to plan through how the Americans might think. If they became aware of the products I was making, where would they look for them? In nice clean premises? Or in the back of a souk? Should I try to hide my activities behind locked doors or carry out work in the open? It was hard to think like this because we have grown up in a culture of hiding everything behind walls from Saddam's security men. But the Americans peer over walls with their airborne surveillance, and there are Iraqis who are happy to tell them which walls to look over. Worse, there are Iraqis happy to betray other Iraqis if there is the prospect of making money. I needed a place the Americans would not think to look. I did not want to hide out of sight. That can be too dangerous. I wanted to hide in the open.

With my new money I was able to sit and watch, drinking coffee and observing how the Americans worked. Those soldiers are just boys. They are careful to stay on the main streets and never go too far from their tanks and armoured personnel carriers. In the past they would never leave their vehicles, but that is beginning to change. There are many more of them patrolling the streets. Nervous. But walking and talking. I cannot blame them for being nervous. But there are some soldiers we do not see. They come out of helicopters in the dark. I had to think about them. It was best to avoid working at night. And I had other things to contend with right then as I sat and sipped sweet coffee in a shady lane with a good view down the street.

'You are working now?' My companion who asked the question was still out of work. I had been buying him coffee for a week. He was careful with his question, for any of us could be working for anybody these days. But such caution is built into the Iraqi DNA. We are born to be careful. I looked at him for a long time. He shrugged and held my gaze.

'Maybe I can help, that is all.'

'Help with what?'

'Whatever you are planning to do. You have money now. Someone is paying you. But so far, I see you only walking and talking. And drinking coffee.' His laugh was tinged with nervousness.

I sipped some more coffee and watched the lane. Then I gambled. 'Where did you go to school, my friend?'

'In Fallujah.'

'And university?'

'I didn't go to university. Why do you ask? Am I a lesser man for that?'

'No, no. Not at all. I simply want you to walk in my footsteps for a moment. I went to school in Baghdad, did my engineering and language studies in Baghdad. I was then sent to do army engineering courses in England and Germany. I was good at what I did. I was commended for my diligence and loyalty.'

'And now you are not?'

I finished my coffee and gazed down the lane into the setting sun. It was time to start walking.

'Come, we will walk and talk. It is safer.'

'Safer than what, eh? Walking is as lethal as riding and riding as lethal as sleeping in my bed at night.'

'Uh-huh, and just as lethal as not having any work either. That is lethal to our families.'

He nodded and we walked towards the river, away from the centre of town.

'Your loyalty is not of any value anymore?'

'I have skills and training and two languages. Maybe even three if I was to spend time practising my German. I can build things. Repair things. Just because I was in the army is no reason to make me one of the lepers in this new country.'

'It was not your army membership.'

'I know, I know. That is what makes all this humiliating and frustrating. No one asked me what I thought. No one asked me my real political allegiance. I was assumed to be untrustworthy. My word was not good enough. I am Iraqi so I am a liar and a thief. That is what they said with their eyes when they signed my papers and stopped my pay. My training and experience mean nothing now. How can I look my sons in the eye? What example am I to them now? I am a man with no honour in my family.'

'They still love you.'

'They still love me. But I am no man if I cannot feed them.'

My friend nodded in agreement. 'You are no man.' He paused. 'But now you are?' He lifted his eyes from the dust and grit in the street to study my reaction.

'If I can find somewhere to safely work then I will be a man again. I am man in their eyes because I now put food on the table. But in my heart I am no man who only takes money without working. I need to work for it. It needs to be honest money. It has to be a colonel's money.'

'*Safely* work?'

'You know I cannot tell you everything. But if I tell you some of the story then you must swear on your grandfather's honour you will not speak of this to anyone.'

'My grandfather?'

'We revere our grandfathers more than our fathers sometimes. I was being careful.' As I need to be in everything right now.

He smiled at me, a half-hearted, hesitant smile. 'I am doing this with no knowledge of what I am getting into. But I am going to do this to help you, my friend. And to honour my father and my grandfather.'

'They are both dead. You know you will join them before you pose a risk to my family. I don't care how many prayers we have attended, or coffees we have sipped, job queues we stood in or generators we stole. You know I will do that?'

He nodded and looked at the ground before gazing out over the wind-rippled river. 'I know that. But I am in need too, and I may just be able to help you hide what you want to do.'

'Oh, how might you do that?'

'I trade when I can. When someone has a contract and wants a driver I take my old Russian truck in and out of cities without any problems. I have all the right papers if anyone bothers to check these anymore. I have access to warehouses where we can store whatever you need to store.'

I laughed. 'You are expecting me to be building bombs?'

'What else is there to build and be so secretive about? What else would make you threaten me?'

'You are right. I should not laugh. But I do not need warehouses. I need a good lab bench with an oscilloscope. I need somewhere I can solder in a clean place. Not too clean but clean enough to test and have good control over quality. I want my designs to work. I also need power. Constant power, and water to set up my board etching. And it has to be where no one will suspect me of doing these things. Can you give me all these?'

He said nothing but crooked his finger at me and bade I follow him. We walked in silence for three blocks, watching the crawling traffic, the groups of idle men loitering on corners, and half listened for the whispering prowl of American helicopters. You do not know who is watching. You can never really know if you are being watched. So just walk normally and never rush.

Soon we were picking over a pile of bricks from a broken-down section of wall. On the other side was a schoolyard.

'Can you teach physics?'

'I know physics, but I have never taught.'

'But could you teach high school students? My cousin is the head teacher here. He is trying to get this school functioning properly again. He needs more teachers. He has some, but many have fled and are too frightened to come back after the looting. They are not yet convinced they will be protected.' He paused.

My friend is a decent man. He was warning me of the insecurity that came with the job. Would I mind? I nodded and he went on. 'Those teachers who stay cannot afford to teach. The school has no money. So they have to sweep streets. Or cook. Or clean. Or travel out of town to find work.'

Now I realised what my friend was suggesting, as I climbed down the small mountain of cascading, broken bricks and walked into the yard.

'Let's have a look at the science lab. I think you will find it will suit your needs.'

We pushed into a hall through open-framed steel doors. A handful of children looked up from the other end of the corridor, but they made no attempt to speak to us. The classroom was three doors down, past litter and shattered timber, bullet gouges in walls, past black and tarred blood stains, which I tried to avoid looking at. Strangely, in this unused classroom, every pane of glass was still in its window frame. I cannot explain that. But sliding doors from cabinets had been wrenched from their tracks and chairs were missing. The benches had been more difficult to steal. A fine layer of gritty sand and dust covered anything left behind. We crunched our way past the front bench and through an open doorway to a laboratory prep room with work benches and steel cabinets, locks broken but repairable.

'There is power?'

My friend shrugged. 'We can find out. There is lighting so I think there would be power.'

'How many classes would I need to teach?'

'I will ask. But my cousin needs as many teachers as he can get. I am sure you can teach any classes you want.'

I met my friend's cousin three days later. He was typical of the Iraqi who assumes a motive other than the one spoken about.

'I want no trouble. This is a school, you know.'

'I am here to teach physics. And to keep my own mind busy.' He had asked after my credentials and was worried someone with so many courses and degrees and international training would not really want to teach. Under the old regime all of those qualifications spelled a different agenda and he would have been right to suspect me then. But I did not intend harm to the school. I wanted a safe place to work.

'I do not understand why you do not want pay.'

'I would like to be paid one day. Keep a tally and pay me when you can. If my children can join these classes that will be payment for the present time.'

He nodded, but I could see he was not happy with the arrangement. I took hold of both his shoulders and looked him in the eye.

'I will come here and teach. I will give you no trouble. If I can help in this small way by getting our children back in the classroom then I will be content. And if at any point you do not like me here, you tell me. I will be told once and I will never come back. Is that acceptable to you?'

He smiled a tight smile. 'Thank you. I will have the room cleaned and ready for you next week. You should take the science book with you to see what has to be taught.' He handed me a tattered, hard-bound volume dated 1986. These students were going to get the basics.

* * *

Every nation has its Messenger; then,
When their Messenger comes, justly
The issue is decided between them and
They are not wronged.

It was cool in the mosque and the men who crowded around were not paying too much attention, each lost in his own thoughts. The message was a favourite of this imam. It was not inflammatory and he used it to assure his flock their lives would return to normal. I think he used it out of context, but who were we to argue? This was a time of solitude and peace and quiet and reverence and fellowship. And his message was of peace. There were no firebrands here preaching hate against the Americans or other infidels. As I made to leave and was straightening my clothes I felt something placed in my pocket but ignored it until I was safely behind the locked gate of my house. Another packet of Winstons containing a short message to meet at the same coffee shop after evening prayers the following day.

It was dark when I arrived. I was very careful in the way I approached, just as I always was. You see, you have to be on alert but not look like you are on alert. Can you do that? It is very difficult to know how you look when you are nervous. But you cannot let your guard down. As I walked the street towards the café I was watching the cars that were slowly trawling up and down. I was watching to see if they were driving with purpose. Some looked like people returning from work. Some were young men driving with nothing to do. Yes, even in the middle of a war there are young men who will get in their cars and drive just to fill in the time. I was usually not too worried about the cars that were moving, although I did want to see the drivers, and like all Iraqi people I was careful about fast new cars with darkened windows that speared into the suburbs from nowhere and vanished with members of our families, most likely never to be seen again. I have been lucky. Maybe because of a good record in the army, but I never had trouble from those vehicles.

It was the parked cars that were the vehicles I watched most carefully. The ones left out on the street are the ones to be cautious and wary about. We have had no car bombs in my suburb, but one day that will happen. I watched the young men who drove. I watched all the men who drove. Once you could be sure a family man with his children in a car was not delivering a bomb. But now in this Gehenna we call home, men blow up their children too. Or maybe a stranger's child is blown up with them. Children! May Allah be merciful to us, but I fear we do not deserve any mercy from Him for these terrible things we invent.

I stepped from one kerb to the other as I walked up the street in the hot, dusty air and watched the shadows clustered on corners or under lights. Sometimes I heard music from behind walls but no laughter or talking. Just silent shadows under butter-yellow lights, shifting in and out of the dark and watching me walk my zigzag walk. Every now and then a shadow would drift towards me. Then it would recognise me and with a lift of the chin signal to me to continue. They too were on edge. Watching and waiting. By the time I reached the café I was wound up very tight, as they say. I needed a hot drink to calm me down. But even here I was careful.

Five or six men were drinking under the glare of the naked light bulbs. The night was still hot and the breeze lifted the dust and dirt of dead civilisations into the corners and crevices, draping our clothes in a drab dun colour and coating drinks before they could be put to our lips. Saleh greeted me as he wiped the grit from the table top before I sat down. He held my gaze for longer than he should have and I worried what that could mean. But nothing further was said and he moved away as my contact bulldozed into the shop and crashed into his seat. Avoiding all the usual polite greetings, he assaulted me with his mouth.

'I thought you were working for us? You took our money!'

This was not a friendly man.

'You told me to find somewhere safe to work, no?'

'Yes. So why are you teaching at the school instead of finding somewhere to work?'

It was the first hint that Halim was not thinking too clearly about what I was being asked to do. He was alert and dangerous and full of ideals and passion and was clearly possessed of a desire to fight someone. I thought then that it was the Americans. I would now call him a crusader, perhaps, but not a leader. An effective lieutenant, skilled in the weapons and waging of war, caught up in the clanking and steam and bustle of battle. Ask him what city was to be taken and he could tell you. Ask him how to get there and he would be perplexed for an answer. A lieutenant, to be sure, but not thinking about how he was doing what he was doing, and that could make him dangerous. Very dangerous. It was too early to understand him completely but I knew better than to mock him. It might be the last thing I do.

'I am to build some electronic devices and I have to do so in a place which is not suspicious to the Americans. The school has a laboratory I can use. It has power and running water which I need to make the boards. I do not think the American tanks and helicopters will shoot at it. It seems like a very safe place to me. And I have a good explanation as to why I am there. Do you not approve?'

The dark face blanked into nothing by shadow, but his teeth flashed in a stiff smile. 'I approve. This is a good plan. I like it. Look out for my notes. They will tell you what to do.' With that he finished his coffee, stood up and strode out without looking back. I paid Saleh, picked up the packet of Winstons Halim had left behind and followed him out some minutes later.

5

Malik

My name is Malik and I am a new man. Today I sold three shirts. They were pale green. That is one good thing. A new American soldier is on the roadblock. He hangs his rifle over his shoulder. Today he held his palm up and smiled from under his sunglasses. They all hide behind their sunglasses. But he smiled and did not point his rifle at me when he wanted me to stop. So two good things happened to me today. When I got home I heard another good thing. My son has had no science teacher for so long. Today he has a new one. A man who knows about science. A teacher who made experiments with paper clips and batteries. My boy thinks he is a clever man. Today he also learned some English words. Just for fun. My boy is excited about this man and wants to be like him. One day I hope Imaad will be able to travel in and out of this country unhindered. He will use his English to talk to an Englishman in England. Even better, he will speak English to an Englishman who is happy to visit Iraq. And not just to visit Iraq for business, but to visit Iraq like people visit Paris. Or Rome. I would like to go to those places one day. Just to have a look. Just like other people can.

So this evening I am at home feeling like a new man. Aha, I know, I have already told you that. Such a simple thing but I am so uplifted. I had forgotten how a little success can make you feel able to climb mountains. I need to be reminded daily of this. I forget to remind myself and each day I was becoming a sadder and sadder man. When I turned the corner into my street I was reminded I could be happier again. So four good things today! Life is good.

What was that reminder? One of my neighbours is a successful businessman. Even during the war. So he can pay for cleaners, a cook and some guards. They are all part of his big family and even the family of the street, for the guards from a number of houses mingle at the front and keep an eye on the street for us all. One of the guards found some puppies and brought them home for the children of his boss. The puppies are playful and they become dirty when they scamper in the dust. When I drove into the street this afternoon the big guard and the little boys were washing the dogs in a bucket of soapy water out on the street. It has been a hot day. The dust of our deserts lies on the leaves of the trees and weighs them down. I think it makes the day even hotter. The dogs, I know, are dusty and panting, heads down, ears drooped and tails listless. They pad through the dust and cast themselves with a weary flop into the nearest shade. Now, they do not mind being in the bucket. But while still wet they flop to the cool earth in the shade of a dusty tree. Dust turns to mud. So the boys pick them up and put them back in the bucket. Then the boys are dirty and the dogs clean. Around and around they went. It made me laugh.

All these ordinary people make me laugh and glad to be Iraqi. They are living in a war, but now they do simple things full of pleasure and we all laugh. Even the cooks and guards strive to keep the rhythms of life beating normally. They make it possible to stay sane. I looked up the street and saw a puppy being washed and covering everyone in mud and water, and a family laughing, and neighbours opening gates to join in the merriment, and I knew we could come out of this war. Sadly it will not be with all our neighbours. I hope and pray it will be with my family and Fatimah. I know in my heart it will be with my family. And I pray it will be with my friendly neighbours, who are all living on the edge every day. These are real people who do not say they deserve anything special. They do say they want a chance. Deserving and a chance are different things. People who say they deserve something sit still. People like the guards and cooks who say they want a chance work hard to make that chance come about. I work hard for that chance too.

As I left the dogs I glanced up to see Apache helicopters float through the sky. How well we have come to know these aircraft after they have patrolled our skies for so long. Everyone in this town knows their planes. We were all trained to identify those owned by Iran and Israel. This is not a war movie here, with thundering sound effects – these helicopters are silent. They look like they fly lazy. But they speed up and turn without warning, which frightens me. As I watched them in the sky, a loud boom echoed in the west. I saw no smoke. I didn't need to. I knew what it signalled. It is a sound like no other and it caused me to shudder and think, 'Who's had a nice day like mine ruined by a madman?'

I hear later that a suicide bomber has killed eight people at a police post. The news headline is not just a number. It is as though one of my family has been part of that incident. Each explosion has a real impact. It hurts us all. We feel the pain even though we behave as if these explosions are normal. People like the cooks and cleaners who work in our street have died in that explosion. People like me who sell shirts. People with children who need to go to school. People who still need their fathers, their mothers, their cousins and all their family around them. Children should be able to play in the street and bring home stray dogs, like kids in other places do. Yet even though these explosions rip through our neighbourhoods, I still see our citizens ignore the terrible sounds and wash puppies. I am glad to see these things, for it tells me how strong we are. These people make *me* feel strong.

I fight my curiosity. I need to go onto the roof to see what has happened. What damage has that bomb inflicted? And where was it exactly? That is how my head works. I want to know. But dinner and the family come first. I have bought some sweets with the shirt money. It is good to spend money other than from the dwindling store of cash hidden behind the tiles in the bathroom. Did you know money can grow mould? I didn't either until I started hiding it.

After dinner I go up to the roof. The sun is a bronze disc low in a still sky. The wind has dropped but the dust still hangs in the hot air and makes for orange and red sunsets. I feel the beat of unseen helicopters. They must be passing close by but the throb fades as quickly as it swells, leaving me to an eerie silence. I brush off the outdoor lounge chair and settle down with my glass of water, which is already sweating drops into the dust. I have little time to myself before my son arrives at the top of the stairs and peers through the door into the dusky evening. I watch him look around then walk over to the wall that surrounds the rooftop and stops him from falling two storeys to the ground. But it is not a good idea to have your head visible for too long and after a few moments I ask him to sit with me.

'School was good?'

'Yes.'

I laugh. Children only tell you what they want to tell you.

'Your mother says you like your new teacher.'

He screws up his face and draws patterns in the dust with his finger. 'Mamma talks too much.'

'But only to the people she loves.'

'It is still too much.'

'So what does this teacher do?'

'He teaches us science. He knows a lot of science.'

'But you have had other science teachers before.'

'Yes, but this man tells stories. He was in the army once. He told us what it was like when he first joined the army. He made us laugh when he told us how bad he was at marching. I march better than him.'

'Ha, yes, you do march well, but marching is not easy for some people. When I did my training some men never got it right. They made it easy for the rest of us because the instructors always yelled at them, not us.'

'You never told me you were in the army.'

I could not tell him of my living nightmare of fear and pain in the trenches. Of my secret hope that I might inflict the same on my fellow men, even if they were from Iran. So I lie.

'Only for a few months. I did my training then got a sickness that put me in hospital. I was so weak I was asked to look after stores, but later I was finally allowed to leave. I got the sickness from cutting my foot on rusty steel. So I do not think I can really say I was in the army. Not like your science teacher. What did he do?'

'I don't know. He said he was there for many years. He told us about tanks and trucks and airplanes. He knows about electrics. He knows lots and lots about everything. He has even been to other countries.'

'Oh, do you know what countries?'

'I cannot remember them all. He did say England.'

'Do you know where that is?'

He shook his head so I leaned over and drew a map in the dust, showing Europe and Britain. 'Here it is. It is a long way to go to England. Do you know anything about England?'

'They play good football. Some of my friends talk about playing football with them, earning lots of money.'

'Yes, you could earn lots of money with England. But you have to be very, very good. Lots of players from all over the world play in England.'

'I could play there. I am very good.'

'Yes, you are, you are very good,' I agree as I tousle his hair. 'But how good is your science?'

'If I study hard with this new teacher I am sure I will be very good. He showed us how electricity works today. We made a light come on and then we learned how to switch it on and off. I could set up a new light in the house now, Baba.'

I have a vision of a small boy killing himself with the main house power as he tries to make a new circuit for us. 'You could do that, my boy, but you need a special permit from the government.'

'Why?'

'So they know you know enough not to kill yourself. Electricity in houses is different from the classroom – it can kill you.'

He is silent for a moment. 'So what I was shown is useless?'

'No, no, nothing like that. What you were shown was the first step. Ask your teacher more and listen and listen, and soon you will be able to fix the house. But not today. Now, off to bed. It is too late to be up here wasting time with me.'

He smiles. 'No, Baba, it is good up here. It is too hot down there. And it is good when I see you are happy.'

'You think I am happy, eh?'

'You were happy looking at the puppies. You do not often smile at the end of the day.'

'You notice too much. But you are right. I worry about our business. And I worry about us all being safe. I worry about you walking to and from school. I worry about your school. I worry there are no teachers. But I am pleased about the news from your mother that you have a new science teacher. He sounds like a good man.'

'He is good, but not as good as you.'

'Now I know you want something,' I tease. 'Off to bed.'

I have allowed myself to get lost up here in the soft night. A shower of sparks drops from the sky in slow silence, bright white, sometimes with a hint of yellow and pink. They are flares dropped by the helicopters that hunt through the dark sea of the sky. Those helicopters are silent and invisible. But people say they can see through the night as if it is day. It would not be a good idea to try and attack them, or commit a crime relying on the night for protection. Sometimes I hear the swish of a helicopter as it slips overhead. They do not beat or throb unless they are very close, and then only for a second or two. So I am careful how I move at night. All an observer would see is a man on a sun chair, looking into the night and not doing anything that might prompt them to shoot at me. I think doing something crazy could get me killed.

I am content. All the bright things today tell me many more good days are possible, despite the thundering blasts that tear at us. Baghdad is becoming a better place. I will not be too hopeful, but maybe there is a chance my children will have a safe city one day. I watch another shower of man-made stars drift to the ground before I go downstairs for the night. Someone up there is watching our city. Hopefully we will sleep safely again tonight. Hopes and prayers, and these Americans working for us make me feel very alive. Yes, I am happy to be alive.

6

Aadil

Is that dictaphone still off? There is not a second recorder anywhere? In your phone? No?

Good!

The books you promised, they are here?

Good.

You are being careful with what you write?

You nod but I still worry. I am chained here like a dog, lying in my own dirt, hosed down by freezing water once a day. You sit on a nice little canvas stool and cross and uncross your neat slacks, tipped off with shiny leather shoes, then cross and uncross your arms, and then take too few notes. You make me wonder who you fear. And you make me wonder how you remember all I am telling you. Or is it that *everything* is recorded? I cannot tell. I am told nothing and the guards are young and ignorant and fearful. Fearful of us, of this place, of these bars, of the stench. Or of their awful discovery that they are capable

64

of becoming Satan, with the power to dispense evil over those of us in these cages? Is that your fear too? Is it that you are frightened of my contagion? That in me, you will see how fragile is the thread holding us over the maw into which you secretly wish to drop so you can taste evil for yourself? The taste of options, of choice, of forbidden fruit. We are not so removed from Adam in this, you know, are we? You look at the floor. Hmm, you are not so different from me, are you now? Do I continue? Or is the ordinariness of my descent into the pit warning you off? Have the guards loosen my cuffs and I will continue.

Thank you. As you already know I had been instructed to heed the messages in the Winston packets. So that is what I did. Inside the next packet was a note which contained a simple instruction and an abbreviated list of capabilities. I burned it straight away, wondering even as I lit the match if this loose security was designed to incriminate me if the Americans uncovered what we were doing. But I realised whoever was paying me had no engineers guiding them. I was now that engineer, and so they gave me a request for what they wanted me to design, rather than a design itself.

They asked for two trigger devices, one straightforward, the other very difficult. The first one was to be managed by a cell phone, which in itself is not so hard. But the design had to have multiple numbers. They wanted one phone to arm the device and also to disarm it. They then wanted a second phone to trigger the explosion. Using two phones was one way to protect against random or accidental detonations, and also a way to help keep your activities covert. None of what they wanted in this first design was beyond my skill, although they demanded the communications be encrypted. That would be difficult and made no sense to me. I would need the help of the telephone company to do that.

The note also instructed me to design a second type of trigger device. The instruction was broad. It was to be a radio transmitter and would use a frequency-hopping chipset to protect the signal from interference and electronic countermeasures. I preferred this approach because it offered advantages over the phone-based trigger, mainly because it avoided the phone companies, which could prevent calls from going through. The transmitter and receiver, I thought, would work if we had the right chipsets. But I knew getting those components would be difficult. I could not just buy them from a local electronics store. They are very controlled items. And unlike the phone-based triggers, a transmitter could be quickly detected and located by the Americans, so whatever I made would have to be disposable. A one-time-only device. And how powerful? Maybe one or two watts, about as powerful as a small walkie-talkie radio. That would make the transmitter small. But it would also make it easier to stop the signal. The Americans easily blocked signals just by drowning them out. Even their armoured cars have devices which drown all electrical signals except their own when a convoy is driving through a hostile area.

I wanted to speak to Halim about these things. He needed to know the pluses and minuses of these triggers, but I had no way of contacting him. So far, he had initiated all of our meetings.

I puzzled over how to meet Halim, then it dawned on me that he had already given me the solution. The next evening I left an empty packet in place of the one Halim had left. My wife cleaned it away many times but eventually the return packet contained a note with the name of a popular clothing store.

I was easing along the rows of trousers touching clothes I had no intention of buying, feeling very nervous when Halim appeared on the other side of the rack.

'You have a problem?' he asked.

'Only that I have no way of contacting you. But I also have some questions.'

'You cannot contact us. But the packet is a good idea.'

'No, it's not. My wife wonders why it is always out there.'

'Okay, we will think of something else. Your questions?'

'How do I get these chipsets?'

'We will supply them.'

'How?'

'We will package them up and send them to the Science Department at the school.'

'Okay, that will work. But will they come with all the specifications?'

'Yes.'

'I need you to understand this. These chipsets will be very delicate and sensitive. Some manufacturers design features into them to track their use. Others design features to ensure they fail if they are not set up properly. Please make sure these chipsets do not have these features and have instructions which help me get around any security barriers.'

He nodded.

'Do you need to write this down?'

He glared at me.

'Okay. Please ensure the instructions are in Arabic or English. German is okay too. They are useless to me in Chinese or French. And even more useless if they are in English translated by a Chinese computer.'

He nodded again.

'My second question. Do I buy the other components from the address you gave me? Are there trusted suppliers? I think some of these parts will attract the security forces.'

'We have people we trust. They regularly import special goods by truck from Jordan which are well hidden from the authorities. Our people are scattered all over the city in small shops that do not attract attention. Start with the address I gave you. Others will be added as you need them. Is there anything else?'

'Yes. My third question is the hardest. Do you know how difficult it will be to use a phone-based system without using the telephone company? I can design some clever devices but they will track us very quickly. Worse, the Americans can just take the network down if they suspect anything.'

'We know these things.' He fidgeted with the clothes and his impatience was barely in check.

'And you still want a design using them?'

'Yes.'

'I prefer the security of a direct transmission.'

'Design and test both. We will be in touch.'

With that he selected a pair of trousers and walked out of the shop, dropping some dinars on the counter as he went. I followed him a short time later. He had not made me comfortable. The cell-phone solution would be indiscriminate. They could explode at any time. A wrongly dialled number might detonate the device in the owner's hands. That is why they wanted multiple numbers, but accidents could still happen. Yet they were paying me, so I walked to the school thinking about how I would do this.

In class I was no longer a colonel. But the boys thought I was. There is no quicker way to get the attention of twelve-year-old boys than to tell them army stories. They tittered and cocked their heads at me and leaned forward in their chairs as they listened to my yarns. They took notice because there had been no classes for so long. Even in their immaturity they understood they had been missing something important. They wanted to learn and I found I enjoyed the teaching. They were eager students and they helped me become a good teacher.

They paid close attention to the lessons. We built simple light circuits. We built batteries. We designed and built coils then put power into them and measured resistance. They loved the explosions of wire heated to an orange glow. There were some small finger burns but no parent contacted the school to complain. When people die every day on the streets, when the grey flesh of neighbours is visible on the blackened stalks of their shattered bones lying in the street, who is going to complain about small burns? The children are alive and not maimed. And in class. These are the main things parents think about. We built filter circuits and simple amplifier circuits and they soaked up the instruction.

But I soon found the most important lessons were the ones that had nothing to do with physics. These were the lessons when the class was subdued and they wondered aloud why their brothers, cousins and other family members had died. Why the Americans were on our streets. Why Saddam, the protector of the nation, had been hanged. Some of these questions they were not able to ask their parents. Some had no parents. They got their information from the street. It was not always useful or true information and they were confused. They loved Iraq. That is good. They hated the Americans. That can be good but not always. It only helps to hate your enemy if you know why you hate him. Blind hatred is pointless. We need to know why we fight. I told the boys the Americans are other men like them. I told them that if they are to fight, then they must fight them with their heads, not with their hearts, for their hearts will betray them, and they will come to love the killing. Then I remembered we were in a classroom and killing is not what I was supposed to be talking about. I asked the boys to turn to page seventeen and started a discussion about alternating current. I recognised their reluctance to move on from martial things. I was a boy not so long ago.

7

Malik

I first met Saleema at the hospital in Fallujah. The hospital is on a bend of the eastern side of the Euphrates River, near one of the bridges of that city. I was on a bus trip when we had an accident on the bridge and I went to the hospital. Saleema was a nurse in Fallujah. Her family lived in Baghdad so she travelled between the two cities, usually staying at the hospital quarters if she was busy, but coming home when her rosters allowed her. It's not such a long trip. I was very weak in my head when I saw my wound and lay down. When I woke she was washing my forehead, and in her tranquil way she assured me my leg would heal. After I disgraced myself by being sick in a bowl she went away. That is what the family found so amusing. That she was stronger than me was a reason for much laughter at my expense. But it was her steadiness in that hospital that first stopped my heart. And then her dark eyes, which she would cleverly make up with rich, earthy colours. It seemed that she could put a calming magic into me when I looked into that face. Soon I was not able to think straight, and even when the leg was repaired my mind was distracted. I was sure she would not be interested in a man who was scarred and who would be sick at the sight of his own wound, and I thought she would never come back. But she saw me every day until I was sent home a week later.

For many months after I left hospital I wrote letters and spent a Persian ransom taking bus trips to Fallujah. But this weak Malik of a man stayed away from her parents until I met them at a family gathering. It was a friendly picnic on the banks of the river, under date palms and not very far from the traffic circle near my shop. People do not do these things anymore and the grass grows long in the parks, catching the wind-blown rubbish. In the days of the dictator we were careful about what we said, but we did not have to be careful about how we lived. Now I do not have to worry so much about what I say, but I have to be very careful how I live. When the dictator was in his palaces, we could be Shia and Sunni sharing the same bed and bringing up our children as we saw best. But we brought them up to keep their thoughts to themselves. We can still live as Sunni and Shia but now there are some of each who attack and even kill the other. So many of our Sunni neighbours are now gone, which is very sad. I do not think we have to worry about the Americans. We have to look out in case it's another Iraqi trying to kill us.

I saw today something that will help explain what I mean. It showed me the sort of place Iraq can become and I want to share it with you. It was something I saw from my roof. Actually, there are two stories. Let me tell them both. The first story tells you something about what we were. The second story tells you why I hold out hope for my country. I prefer the second story.

The first story is about me. I was on my dusty lounge on the roof and it was the Holy Day. I was not in the mosque but I had prayed. As I sat in the blue-dry heat of the middle of the day and listened to the hum of city traffic I heard shouts in the distance. They sounded like the orders I once obeyed when I was in the army. There were more shouts, commands this time. They were coming closer. Silence. Then more orders. Many orders and many men, coming in my direction.

I began to worry. Do I get my family to the middle of the house and unpack the AK-47 from behind the refrigerator? I do not know. Then the shouts and orders were very close and I could hear other men communicating with each other as they approached. It is a very dangerous thing to look over the top of the wall around the roof but I took a chance. On the other side of my street is a large park full of eucalyptus trees. They say their scent is beautiful in the heat of Australia but I have never smelled them here. In the heat of Iraq they are covered in a thick layer of desert sand and dust and there is no scent. Just the odour of ancient dust filled with the dead voices of Assyrians and Babylonians and Greeks and millions of others who have moved through here since God created Eden. I think that was His joke, putting Eden here, for He teases me with His idea of paradise in this part of the world. But I was in no mood to think of God, for through the grey green of the drooping leaves of the eucalypts I saw men in formation, moving like shadows towards me.

Urgent commands got louder. Through the trees I now saw AK-47-armed, headband-wrapped men dashing forward. I had to decide whether this was a training exercise or whether I should be making my family safe. I was about to run downstairs when an order was shouted and the men stopped running, stood still and started taking out their water bottles. How foolish I felt. This was an exercise for one of the new army or police units, probably being trained by the Americans.

I remembered this was how we used to be. Always worried about any strange activities by men in uniform. Then I thought some more and realised this fear was ingrained in our culture. Uniforms are not to be trusted. This is not how it should be. That is the first story. See, we distrust people put in charge of protecting us.

If the first story tells you what we were, this other story tells you what we might still become. God willing. But first, let me ask you a question. Can you tell a Sunni from a Shia if they are dressed the same? I do not think you can. Can you tell the difference if they have no clothes? That is harder still. If, then, you see a group of men working in shorts, wearing work boots and maybe hats, can you tell the difference? Not at all.

Today on my roof, towards the end of the day, I heard other men's voices make a very different noise from the training soldiers. Squeals of terror mixed with laughter and the shouts of about twenty men. I got up from my outdoor lounge, leaving sweat glistening in the sun. At the wall I peeked over with some caution. What I saw below made me join in the pleasure too. A construction company had come into my neighbour's yard and was pouring concrete. The men were in T-shirts and shorts and there were Sunni and Shia and even Kurds all working together. I only know this because my neighbour has told me. For many days the empty site next door has been busy with large, muscular, tanned men with black hair matted across their shoulders and chests, pouring concrete, shaping steel and sweating rivers in the sun. The work is almost complete and painters had arrived to paint the floor.

As I looked over the edge, these tough bearded men were squealing like six-year-old girls as they tried to get out of the way of a lizard. One of the men had caught the reptile and was chasing his friends with it. They flapped their hands in horror, shrieking and trying to climb up on the trucks to get away. If you had any ideas about how a construction worker might behave, then they would vanish if you had seen these men. And, at the end, the lizard was gently let down in a cool pool of water that had collected when they had hosed the concrete clean. The lizard was no doubt frightened by his adventure with these big men but he still had his life. In a land of random violence it was a surprise to see the lizard waddle in the water and not get stamped to death under a worker's boot. I went back to the lounge with a light heart. This had been a good thing to observe and gave me hope for our future.

So I tell you these stories. One of what we were and one showing what I pray we will routinely become. The lizard story is to tell you that all of us can work together and play together. With the work finished the men relaxed, and I could hear them joking with each other and talking about their families. We all have families and things we share in common.

It is late now. The sun has let down in a dusty sky, though the heat remains. I hear a crunch of grit and look over to see Saleema walking across from the doorway, drink in her hand. Her niece Fatimah follows.

'What was the commotion from over the fence earlier?' Saleema inquires.

I tell them about the lizard. Saleema laughs, her eyes twinkling and her teeth flashing in the dusk. I never cease to marvel at how her face lights up when she laughs. Her cheeks are tinged with red and her skin glows.

Both women take off their shawls and shake out their hair before sitting down on chairs beside me. 'These men are not so tough, then?' Fatimah proposes as she sits down, taking care not to overbalance.

'I think they are tough. Very tough. They are too tough for you. I do not think they would be proper for you.'

She giggles. 'You think they are too tough for me? Are you sure you know what type of man I need?'

'I am family. I think I know. Or, if I am honest, I want to believe I know what is best. And it is not one of these men. Their hearts are mainly good, but their hearts have been so roasted in ovens they are crusted hard. Their hearts beat but they are not supple. They might love you but will never tell you so.'

She arches her eyebrows at me in that mocking way she has. 'Ah, my brother, and you always tell Saleema that you love her?' Too late, I know I have trapped myself and am conscious of Saleema's calm but bemused gaze on me.

'True, true, not enough. But I am sure more than these rough men would ever tell their wives. Come, Fatimah, you should be loved by a man who seeks earnestly to find treasure and does not settle for fool's gold but only the real thing. You want a man who will carefully track down a rare orchid, not settle for a mountain daisy.'

'They are both beautiful. You are being tough on the daisy,' remarks Saleema.

'It is true they are both beautiful. But one requires a man to study hard what he is looking for and to not settle his heart until he has found it. The other is stumbled upon every day. It is beautiful but it is common. The common daisy requires no testing of the heart.'

'You do like talking about flowers,' scolds Saleema.

'What can I say? They teach us so much. Fatimah is a rare and beautiful flower who must be treasured by the right hunter of rare flowers, not the common man stumbling through the hills on a picnic.'

Fatimah smiles and reaches over to rest her hand on my shoulder, something she can only do on this roof. 'You are a strange man but a good one, I know. You are protecting me like a brother or like a father. I love you like a sister or a daughter for that.' She withdraws her hand and places it demurely in her lap, then drops her gaze to the ground.

We sit still, the three of us, and I feel her sorrow for a moment. 'You are lonely, I see. Even though you are with our family.'

She nods slightly without lifting her gaze. When she speaks it is barely a whisper. 'What happened is no different from many families in this country. But I do not wish to endure the same hurt again. Can you imagine being a wife and losing your husband for no sensible reason? Can you imagine being a mother and losing your children for a cause that escapes any rational mind? Saleema and I talk about this and she knows I mean no disrespect. But how can I do this thing – love and be loved – and not lose? I do not know.'

Saleema murmurs something soothing, but I am silent. It is a conversation we have on occasions. I want to assure Fatimah that we can mend ourselves if we love, especially in these times. But my words will only be met with a firm shaking of her head and a glare in her green eyes. We will only hurt each other with our arguments. I know that the more hurt there is, the more we need to love and to be a normal family. If we all do this then one day we will win and emerge a civilised people. If we give in and refuse to love then we all lose. There is something in our niece that is afraid to love and my heart aches for her loss. For that is what has happened. She has loss because she will not love. She has emptiness and loneliness in the early watches of the oven-hot night when she lies awake wondering what it might be like to have her own family around her again.

This, I know, is what she thinks as she gazes at the ground. I watch her and love her and feel the sagging weight of this madness on my soul. She is beautiful and fresh and fathomless and untouchable and she is my sister. I know her and her loneliness but I do not know her. Her despair, hidden behind her loveliness, is an obstacle that threatens my ideal of raising each other out of this cesspit. Her soul is the poison to my flower and I feel the petals curl and the stem fold under the emptiness of her heart. But what can I say? I return to safer ground and the subject of the hairy-shouldered construction workers.

'You know, some of these construction workers fought in the front trenches in the war against Iran. But today I heard them forgetting about these things. They come from many tribes but they worked together. And they realised they could laugh together too. Baghdad used to be a place of parties. Maybe we can laugh again. Maybe we can be friends despite our different religions. If a simple thing like a lizard can join us in laughter then we can laugh and unite in other things. We have differences. But they are good differences.'

Fatimah lifts her head and her face softens but says nothing. Now Saleema speaks in that measured way she has when the topic is serious.

'I wish it was as simple as a lizard that would make life safe here again.'

'It is coming normal. You wait. You will see. We will have picnics by the river again. And laugh at lizards.'

She smiles. 'I hope so. I hope we do for the sake of the children. Our children are growing up with a perverse idea of what normal is.'

'You told me the school is now getting some good teachers back. Our son is excited by his new science teacher. It sounds like he is an inspiring man. He has all the boys itching to get to his class each day.'

Saleema frowns. 'Just as long as they are wanting to go because he is a good teacher, not because he is filling their heads full of useless stories.'

I reach over and stroke her hair. 'You worry about the children too much. The boy is learning. He came home and wanted to fix our wiring based on his first lesson on electricity. That is not a story but a useful thing to learn.'

'I know. But teachers the boys like too often want to fill their heads with religion or war. And sometimes both.'

8

Aadil

I had not seen 'Mr Winston' for some time. Suddenly he reappeared, crumpled and tattered on my doorstep, and later that night I met with Halim. We sipped coffee under the same naked light bulbs. Something was agitating him; he was blunt and the meeting was short.

'Next time we meet we want to know about your progress.'

'I have two designs as you requested.'

'Do they work?'

'They work on the test bench. I run test loads on them rather than transmit. I do not want to draw attention to myself. Or to the school.'

'The school does not matter. But you are now dangerous to us. You understand that?'

He did not frighten me. But his tone put me on edge and I was wary. I knew I had to watch him very carefully.

'I understand.'

There was a long, awkward pause as he glared at me. Then he asked, 'How would you test them?'

'Not in the open. I know what the Americans can do when they monitor our electronics. And the phone networks are in the hands of the Americans. If we are to be successful we need to test these in the middle of the city, among all the other electronic noise.'

He nodded. 'Get me the devices, I will let you know.'

'Know what?'

He said nothing but stood quickly and left, disappearing into the crowded night street. I picked up the packet of Winstons, paid for the coffee and went home.

I had worked hard after school hours and between classes. I cleaned the windows of the classroom and put new seals on the doors. I brought in friends who had no work who cleaned and then painted the benches and seats. They put a layer of varnish on the floors. Some found pictures to hang, and one retired army surgeon brought in a plastic skeleton missing three ribs and stood him in the corner. The boys named him Adam. Some of those men continued to work around the school. It kept them busy. Mr Winston helped pay them.

I bought the items I needed from the various shops and stalls which I had been told to contact. No one asked any questions. It helped that all the pieces I needed were the same as those I needed for physics and science lessons. Resistors, capacitors and transistors. The timing chips were the same. The frequency-hopping chipset was the one exotic device I could not buy from the stalls. And nor would I want to buy it locally, even if it was available. Such an extraordinary component would only bring me to the attention of the Americans. I wanted Halim and whoever he was working with to supply them. This was not perfect but if they had been able to avoid the Americans so far then they had a better chance of avoiding them now. Maybe they came from China. Or from France or Italy or Germany. I did not care where they were from as long as I was not compromised when they were handed to me or when I tested them.

I see from your puzzled face that you do not understand. You irritate me sometimes with your naivety. But then I need to remember you did not come down to this prison to hear my story, did you? You came here to see what sort of beast I am. No? The story? I am never so sure about that when you do not follow what I am saying. You were not expecting an engineer in the cage, were you?

Settle down and let me explain. The frequency-hopping chips are very unusual. They are designed to help a transmitter not stay on one frequency. They transmit a little bit of their message on one frequency, then jump to another frequency and transmit a little bit more of the message, then move on to another frequency, and so on. If an enemy finds some of the message on one frequency he will only find a small part and not the whole message. Just to be sure, the message is protected by code. But it is no good if your transmitter can jump all over the place and your receiver has no idea where the message has gone. So I needed a second chipset to go into the receiver and which is married to the first. The second chipset understands the transmitter and where the frequencies are, so it can pick up all the parts of the message and piece them together into a command. Some chipsets are so clever they randomly select a new frequency and transmit that in code to the receiver chipset. The receiver quickly goes there and downloads the message then jumps to the next frequency it is told about and waits for the next piece of data. Even better are the chipsets that have the frequencies and order pre-programmed. If someone is listening and can break the code they still may not know what the next frequency is, so only get some of the message.

You nod. Yes, I agree, they are very clever, and I have told you only a small part of how clever they really are. For example, they can hop thousands of times a second. They are amazing designs. But using them is not fail-proof in this place. Why not? Because the Americans, if they detect a chipset working like this and do not recognise it as their own, well they are inclined to shoot first. And only rarely ask questions. They blast the source of the transmitter and move on. They are very sensitive to this sort of technology being used against them. If they do not understand it they destroy it. It is safer that way for them but highly dangerous for us.

The space behind the classroom had been a teacher's preparation room and was ideal for me as a laboratory.

I spent time working on the basic design and then set up trial circuits on breadboards. I was very careful to ensure nothing was transmitted from an aerial, but that the signals from the design were channelled into an oscilloscope only. After three or four attempts I was happy with a design that appeared to do what I wanted, so I drew the circuit layout, etched it onto the copper board, drilled the board, then soldered components in place. It was a nice piece of work and far too tidy and the workmanship to good for what my employers needed. I take pride in what I do and do it well. I could see the trigger worked when tested on the oscilloscope and was confident the device would perform in the field. I then reduced the size of the design to see if it could function on less power.

The first phone-based trigger was tested on the bank of the river opposite the International Zone. It was a dangerous place to do such a thing. So many American forces patrolled the area, and the local security forces are on extra alert there. But for that reason it is also a very good test environment. We know the Americans have massive electronic monitoring technologies and suppression technologies in downtown Baghdad. If we could get a device to work there it would work anywhere.

I was surprised I was invited to the test, but I should have realised they would want me to be around if something went wrong. Dead men don't talk, do they? And if I had been caught, then I could identify no one except Halim, and perhaps he was expendable too.

I rode my bicycle to the river, as directed, and propped it with dozens of others, all leaning on the low wooden railings that lined the river-bank roadway. I took my newspapers and shoulder bag, sat under the shade of the weeping trees and watched the children play – those children with no parents to warn them about the dangers of playing down there. I had received a slip of paper in the usual way, which instructed me where to go to watch the test. It gave me no idea what I should be watching or listening for, although I guessed there would not be anything so radical as a large explosion. But I was not expecting that one of the bicycles would be the source of the sharp crack and the puff of yellow-grey smoke, which was immediately pulled away from the small tangle of bicycles by the breeze. None of the children paid the noise any attention, and my guess is that they heard nothing over the sound of the wind and the slapping waters of the Tigris. Three hundred metres away the security personnel manning a roadblock gave no sign of seeing or hearing anything.

I waited an hour and enjoyed the afternoon before wandering over and picking up my fallen bike. Looking down into the torn pannier of the neighbouring bicycle I could see the blackened remains of my circuit board. I would have to be careful I did not leave a signature in my design or any other clue that might point to me or to where it was built.

I rode away and tried not to think about what I had seen. I hoped Halim and his friends would not be using my designs in public places. If they were going to be used, then I wanted them used only against the enemies of the people of Iraq, not in places where my own countrymen might be injured or killed.

You have to believe that was true of me, but I see the scepticism in your face.

The next meeting at the café was different from the previous one. Halim was excited, which worried me.

'Your device worked very well. We rang each number in turn and then it triggered. You heard it?'

'I heard it.'

'My boss is very pleased. He wants you to build fifty. Are you able to do this?'

'That depends on how quickly you want them. I also need to be careful about drawing attention to myself. Do not ask me to order large numbers of even ordinary things. That will look unusual.'

'Fifty components will look strange?'

'If I have been buying small numbers, yes.'

'But fifty for a classroom is not so out of place.'

'No, not strange at all. You are right. I can build maybe ten a week if they are to be done properly. And if you are still wanting me to work on the high-frequency device.'

'Ah, yes, when can we test that?'

'That is still a long way off. Each part, the transmitter and the receiver, needs to handle the frequency hopping and to be in sync with the other. Both parts of the trigger are difficult to design and manage. You know, your biggest challenge is going to be the Americans monitoring the airways for this sort of communication. They will know the location of the transmitter almost as soon as you transmit.'

He was still as he listened. His face told me he did not really comprehend these things and he said nothing.

'They might fire a Hellfire at the source of the transmission if they think it is a threat.' He did not smile when I laughed and said, 'That will be one way to see that the device is working.'

'So how do we test it?'

'Do not have an explosion like the bike. That is nonsense. Have a light trip on or simply turn on a television or kettle. But as soon as the Americans become aware there is a frequency-hopping trigger they will do everything they can to block it and destroy the transmitter. This device might make a communication very secure, but it will just as easily bring down Gehenna on you. On us. On us all.'

He did not miss a beat. Consequences were not his concern. 'But that has not helped me understand what we do to have the devices tested.'

'I will build two transmitters. Use one to test the first trigger, but let's have two devices in case the first is discovered or destroyed. The transmitter will not have to send its signal for long but synchronising the receiver and transmitter can take some short periods of time – less than a second – before the message is sent. Those are the dangerous moments when a weapon can be fired at you from somewhere high and unseen.'

He nodded. 'Let me know when you are ready for a test.'

'Okay. I will also get the receiver set up to turn on something simple such as a television or a light. That will require some more time. At least with the receiver we will not need to worry about it being found by the security forces.'

'This is good work. We have never had someone this efficient, or this aware of all the issues. Take care.'

That evening at home I watched the children get ready for bed. They had a meal of fresh vegetables and we had a full tray of cooked rice and goat meat. My wife had bought these things in the market yesterday and had been happily preparing meals since then. Tonight they enjoyed their food as they told each other about their day. The boys who have returned to school are relieved to be children again, not breadwinners. They dare to hope for their education. How different some money makes to our lives. How much pride is put back into the family when the head of the house is able to earn an income.

There were moments when I wondered about what I was doing. These devices were going to be used in a war against the Americans. As long as they were to be used to defeat the enemies of Iraq, then I would build them. But if they were used against believers, then what would Allah say? Could the happiness of my family be justification for the unhappiness of others? What if the

Americans did want us to be free and for us to run our own country? Were we really at war with them?

But other worries entered my head that day. They were worries based on instinct and came from things Halim had said. For a reason I cannot tell you, simply because I do not understand it myself, I had thought Halim was working for a committee. That he had a command structure, like the military perhaps, where a number of people would be responsible for coordinating the work against the enemy. But today he referred to his boss. It was an expression that troubled me. Was there a command structure or was this the head of a tribe he was working for? A tribal elder could also run a military campaign and I would find that acceptable. For the briefest of moments I wondered if Halim was working for the remnants of an intelligence or security group waging its own war. Such a group would usually only work under one leader.

There was another little worry in my head from this conversation. Halim had said they had never had anyone as clever as me, or someone as aware of the issues. Did he think I was a fool? What did he think he was saying? Surely he must know my skills and knowledge could be found anywhere in Baghdad? It made me ask myself again who this Halim really was, and I questioned if he and his fellows really were attacking the Americans. Sadly I did not think this through any further. Perhaps if I had done so I would not be sitting in this cell marked for death and talking to you.

9

Malik

The traffic circle is busy this morning. Drivers are travelling just a little bit faster than usual. Mahrus is his usual welcoming self, but is standing back in the doorway of the shop rather than out on the pavement. I worry I have missed something, so I ask Mahrus directly.

'Is everything okay, Mahrus?'

He shifts slightly and looks around as if he is not very sure. 'Yes,' he replies. 'Yes, I think so.'

'The traffic is different this morning.'

'Yes, maybe the roadblock on the other side of the bridge is not so busy?'

'It is very busy. I came through there this morning. Lots of traffic going very slow.'

'So no problems expected near the roadblock, then?'

'None that I could see. But something is different. Something has everyone worried. Even you, Mahrus, not standing on the pavement like you usually do.'

'I feel something is different. But I do not know what, exactly.'

Staying alive in this city is an uncertain thing. We are foolish men if we think we can control whether we live or die. But we are foolish too if we do not take notice of the warning signs, even if we do not know what those signs are. It is one thing to sense what is typical or not typical in our home streets. It is another thing to sense what is normal in the middle of a city. Mahrus sees or senses everything happening around him. Maybe he has seen something out of place. Maybe he is alert to the pace of the traffic, which might slow or speed up if something is going to happen in a street. A random bomb will not change things. But a planned explosion, designed to attack a convoy or an American patrol, will change what happens in the street, even if the planning is very careful. Somehow people know and they stay away. So the streets stay clear and traffic can get through. Maybe that is what worries Mahrus.

As usual I wipe down the shirt boxes and make sure the lights are working. I sweep the dust from the shop floor, pushing the grit that has accumulated overnight out onto the street, then clear the path in front of the shop. Mahrus still seems wary, and remains hidden in the frame of his door. I put my broom away and stand in my own doorway, leaning there, waiting to see what the day will bring.

Braced for the worst I am surprised when a young man appears from around the corner. He has a piece of paper in his hand which I guess is a shopping list. I watch him approach, looking at the store fronts and peering into some, avoiding others and making his way towards me. It is hard locating a street number – if that is what he is doing. Signs have not been on the streets for many years and our store numbers have long faded off the shopfronts. Mahrus once had brass numbers, but after the fighting started the tiles they were attached to shattered and fell off one dark night and the numbers were swept up in the debris the next day.

The young man walks up to my doorway and I step onto the path to let him inside. I allow him time to look at some shirts before I follow him in.

'I see you know where to find good shirts.'

'A man at the interview office told me I should look at your shirts.'

'The interview office?'

'I have had some interviews for a job with our Ministry of Foreign Affairs. I now have a final interview with higher-ups next week.'

'And they need you to look your best?'

'Yes, they suggested Foreign Office people should be ready to meet their counterparts from other embassies. They do not want us wearing polyester shirts and brown suits.'

I laugh. That is a picture of the Iraqi that is very common. We have our own style of dressing, but our idea of being well dressed is not the same as in London or Paris.

'Well, let's see. Button-downs are still popular in America and wide lapels are favoured by many. The catalogues from my suppliers show the Europeans still look for the sharper and crisper look. We can do that with cotton. It is best not to have too many bold patterns or stripes. But there are many subtle patterns in the material that we can detect. You look disappointed that we should not have patterns, eh?'

'I do like prints, but I think you are right in what you say. The Ministry of Foreign Affairs is supposed to be delivering radical messages dressed in conservative clothes.'

I liked his insight. 'Hopefully not too radical. But maybe messages to the world that we are like other people. That we want to live peaceably. We want our children to be safe. We want to be able to go to school and play with our grandchildren. If you are delivering those messages to the world it will help that you are dressed like them too. If you dress well they will see you appreciate the better things.'

'People should not have to dress like others to get their message heard. Gandhi met world leaders and was well known as a man of the people, and he dressed simply and as an Indian. His message was clear, despite what he wore.'

'Gandhi was not always like that. He started his fight and giving his message as a lawyer dressed in a good shirt and with an old school tie.'

'No? I cannot see him dressed like that.'

'Ask Mahrus about Gandhi. I have told you all I know about Gandhi. Mahrus will tell you more about him. He was a simple, complicated man.'

'Mahrus?'

'No, Gandhi. But so too is Mahrus.'

'Who is Mahrus?'

'My next-door shopkeeper. I think you will like him.'

By now I have selected four very fine white cotton shirts for this young man with the bright eyes and good haircut and insufficient reading. He needs to see the world and he is going to make a difference if he can. I like him.

'These are good shirts. They are my best. Many shirts come from India. But these are from Spain. They are quality-made and more comfortable in hot weather. But they will be good for you in cool weather too.'

'All the same size?'

'All the same size. I will get my measure to make sure my eye is still good. But I think I have the size you need. Yes, yes, go ahead and try one on. No one will see from the street.'

He looks embarrassed. Someone seeing his naked torso is not a problem, but he is still shy about doing that in the open. I glance towards the doorway and the street. I can see Mahrus watching and listening, his lips curled in amusement.

My new customer is pleased with his shirts. He takes all four, pays me with a large pile of dinars, shakes my hand and leaves the shop. He is very happy.

His happiness infects me. Those were my most expensive shirts, taken from the top shelf, and there is more money in my hand than I have seen in nearly one whole year. I try not to get excited. But I have a small swirl stirring in my stomach. I lock most of the dinars in a leather satchel and hide it in a shirt box on the shelves among all the other shirts. Then I take the rest of the money and walk out onto the path.

'My friend, I want to buy some sweets. Some for you and me. Some for my neighbours and some for my family. Then, my friend, I want you to turn on that old coffee maker you have not touched for so long. It is probably rusted into a heap that will not work.'

Mahrus shakes his head and grins. 'No, Malik, I keep it ready for a day like today.'

'You have been watching?'

'Ha-ha. I do not have to watch when I know you so well. A young man came in and paid you cash for all those shirts he walked out with.'

I slap his shoulders. Gently. I cannot help myself. 'Well, then, you and I are going to have some coffee to celebrate the sale I have just made.'

While Mahrus is busy in his shop I walk up the street to an old café that has not been in use for nearly two years. No bomb has exploded near it. It ran out of money when no more people walked down the street. From there I borrow four small steel chairs. They are a mess and one has a bent back. I put them in front of the shop of old Mahrus and go back to pick up a small steel-lattice table. From the back of Mahrus's shop I take rags and a bucket of water and clean the chairs and table. When all that is done I can see the spiced coffee is ready. So I walk to the counter in Mahrus's shop.

'Two coffees and some of those pastries there, please.'

Mahrus starts to protest my purchase.

'I will not listen to this, my friend,' I say. 'Today my fortune is your fortune. My blessing is your blessing. My money is your money.' I hold up my hands and look away to sign that there is no more argument. Then I pay and we sit on the path at the little table and sip our drinks.

We sit in silence, as friends do, and watch the traffic speed past. We sit for five minutes. Then we sit for five minutes more and enjoy a small taste of the old Baghdad. And as we sit there I warm up the thought that crept into the back of my mind as I sold those shirts to the bright young man with his heart set on his new calling. It warms so much it must spill onto my face, for Mahrus eventually asks what the foolish grin is about. I protest that there is no foolish grin, but Mahrus is not to be easily brushed off and I have to confess.

'You know the niece of Saleema?'

He raises his eyebrows over his cup but says nothing. I am forced to plough on.

'Saleema is always telling her to get married. To find a nice man and to have a family. A family will fill the hole in her heart with joy. Sometimes even I have that conversation with her too.'

'You do?' Mahrus is startled.

'Come on, Mahrus, she is family. She to us and we to her. She has no other. Who is to be uncle and father to her about these things if I am not?'

'And I suppose you fill her head with stories of flowers too?'

'They are good stories, Mahrus, very good stories.'

'Of course they are. But you have not explained your foolish face.'

'Fatimah is very well educated. She comes from a good family. She has money. She is careful with her words and guarded in her behaviour. She deserves the very best man, not some fool who is running around this city killing and being violent. She needs a man with an education. A man who will care for her. A man who will provide for her. Properly. I am very sure of this, you know.'

'You talk like a father indeed. But where are we to find such a man? Every father is hunting these men down for their daughters and has given up in despair, settling for lesser mortals.' He smiles as he speaks and I know he can read my innermost thoughts.

'The young man I met today and who purchased those shirts. He is handsome. He has a vision for himself and for his country. He speaks boldly but with respect. This man is a man I think I should introduce to Fatimah.'

'Truly you are a fool. It is in your head and on your face. You would marry up these two people, one you know well and who is family, and this young man who could prove to be the death of us all. You do not know him.'

'True, true, so true, old man. But I have a good feeling about this young man. If he comes back, then let's see what is possible. I will not rush into this but maybe there is hope for joy in the heart of Fatimah yet.'

Mahrus says nothing but holds my gaze as he finishes his coffee. I am satisfied with that. He will keep his counsel and see how things fall. But if I am wrong he will gently prod me with reminders of my foolishness until he or I die. I feel glad. This is a beautiful thing I can do. Fatimah might have the answer to her bitter tears. And maybe, just maybe, I can be the bringer of this joy. We both lapse into silence and enjoy the morning.

Out of nowhere a man strides across the street and surprises us both. He asks for some coffee and permission to sit with us. He has a store on the other corner. All the shops on either side of him are barricaded closed. He sells batteries and torches and small gas cookers imported from Norway. The sort of gas cookers used by people who put packs on their backs and climb mountains, and which are now sought by the people of Baghdad. He also sells radios and TVs, but not so many of these, I think, in present times. Many more instead of the small parts people need to fix the broken ones they have. But there is no community of other shopkeepers around him and his customers stay only long enough to buy his goods then scurry home. Mahrus and I have wondered how he survives on such little trade, but survive he does, like us.

Today he sees us sitting in the street and thinks he would like to drink coffee and talk. His store is in the good hands of his twelve-year-old boy. Yes, his son should be in school. But no, it is not safe to send him from this part of the city yet. How much is the coffee? And can he have some of that *baklava* please?

On the roof of the house tonight I think about this new day. It has been a day like every other. Simple and safe. Mahrus has sensed there was something amiss, but there was nothing wrong. Were his instincts mistaken? I do not think so. I think his instincts are very true. He sensed the changed traffic. He sensed there was something different in the town. But the little piece of normal business we did today was overpowering and he put aside his fears and sat out on the street and ate and drank and talked. Two friends and one stranger. Doing something natural. And a young man in a reconstituted ministry of our country, about to do something new and fresh for us. He visited my store and started a small avalanche of hope. Things are getting better. 'Today the good things are permitted you,' floats into my thoughts, words from the Book and from the imam when he taught me as a boy about what I was allowed to eat and not eat. Today the good things are permitted and they are customers, friends, food and drink and, above all, hope.

10

Aadil

The second test was a failure and it nearly killed me. Not content with the tiny scale of our bicycle test, new plans were put in place. They were to detonate a second device, this time on the route used by supply convoys arriving from Basra to the south. It was a dangerous idea. It made me wonder again what experience these people had. The people I was dealing with had no comprehension how easily the Americans could see us at night. Trying to set up an explosion beside a highway is one way to ensure you are shot from the air, from a long distance away, by an enemy you cannot see. My strong advice against it perhaps helped them to be more careful than they might otherwise have been. But my position was difficult. If I protested too much, these people, of whom I had no real knowledge except through Halim, might think I was not wholeheartedly supporting them. It was one thing to be an engineer and designer, but I knew they wanted my whole being committed to this project. If I was them that would be my expectation. So my objections were couched in a way that looked like expert advice.

As usual it happened over coffee. Late at night. It was a far shorter conversation than I wanted. I am convinced Halim heard only half my warnings and it was this which got us into trouble in the end.

I was as direct as I could be. I told him, 'I know what night surveillance was used against us in 1991. They can fight in the dark. We cannot.'

He had the air of a man who thought I was telling him stories of phantoms and fairies. He laughed.

'I tell you this from my experience in the field. We could not move at night without them seeing us. They use heat detection and they can do that from a long distance.'

'But we will be kilometres from Baghdad. They cannot see us that far away.'

'They can see us from the moon if they want. The point is you never know what they have up there. It is silent. It could be a remote vehicle. Surely you have seen the films from 1991 when pilots could see us from the cockpits of their aircraft. These were not even tools specially designed to hunt us out at night. Yet still they found us.'

'But still we are able to strike.'

'Yes,' I conceded. 'We can strike. They cannot be everywhere at once. But there are a lot of them and there are target areas that are watched very closely. The road from Jordan to Baghdad is one. The road from Basra to

Baghdad is another. If you are lucky you might launch a single attack. But their inevitable counterstrike will mean you never live to fight another day. You have asked for fifty of these things and I suspect you will ask for more than that. You are hoping to fight many days. Well, you need to plan to fight many days as well.'

I sipped my coffee and hoped my voice was not too panicked. I was starting to get frustrated. It was difficult to believe I was dealing with a group who understood so little about the enemy they were fighting. Surely they had done their targeting better than this. Halim was silent for a moment as he stirred his coffee.

'You have seen these things.'

'Not always directly. But when I was a junior engineer our government wanted to purchase surveillance equipment. We looked at American, British, German and French technology. We wanted to understand what was available to us so we could see deep into the rear of the Iranian lines. The Americans took us to a desert area and showed us how easy it was to see soldiers hiding in trenches at night. That technology is now many years old. But each time one of our APCs or T-72s vanished in a bang and a flash in the darkness of the hell that was 1991, it was not by accident that it did so. The Americans and the British could see us as if it was day. We fought with our eyes closed.'

'Hah, our leadership put those weapons in the wrong place and did not attack but hid in the ground. We could have won if we had attacked.'

I glared at him, barely restrained, then took a risk. 'You speak of things you do not understand and parrot something you heard as a boy in a rustic compound that passed for a school. You speak the language of foolish women. If you wish to fight these Americans you need to understand what you fight. If you are going to win you need to do your homework. I thought you had done that with the first test. Now you are showing me you are not so clever with these other tests. I can promise you, the quickest way to Gehenna is to start foraging around on the side of the highway in the early hours of the morning. You will be seen as if in the brightness of day and then you will be dead. You will not even see or hear death coming. The Americans can kill you from five kilometres away and then they might ask questions later. Mostly they will just kill you and never ask questions. You will be like a scene in a video game. Shoot, kill, move on to the next scene. The shooters will not even want to know who you are.'

Was my employment over? Would I be silenced now for knowing too much? I expected Halim would finish his coffee and then return to me at some other time, having asked his superiors about my message, about my commitment and about their next steps. He surprised me.

'If the Americans can see us so well, what do you propose we do to conduct a bigger test?'

'The answer to that is simple. Hide in the open. Conduct the test in a busy area. Set up the device near one of their transport routes. It need not disable anything.

But you can test timing and delay, signal interference and all the other things you want to test, though I am sure these elements are sound. Testing your operations is the key.'

'Hiding in the open. That is difficult.'

'Yes, it can be. But look around at the city. There are numerous new technologies, and new companies installing new technologies. Perhaps you are able to pretend to be one of the new telephone companies. Many small new vans are driving around the city installing and repairing electronic equipment. Steal one of those. Or perhaps you could copy one and use that for your test. Better still, there are cable junction boxes and power junction boxes that could be set up along the route. Have repairmen install what looks like one of these junctions. But it is really a hide for explosives. They have power to them which is helpful. You could only use these two or three times before the Americans made them dangerous to be near. Then you could move on to the next thing. What would a concrete power pole full of explosives do to an American convoy, do you think?'

Halim was leaning forward as he listened. Yet his eyes betrayed nothing. When he spoke I was encouraged to think that perhaps I still had my job. And my life.

'I think we are not using you properly. You have too many ideas about how to do this. Good ideas.'

'They are not new ideas. When the lines of the front around Basra shifted so often, many items were booby-trapped like this. Men died by handling things they should not have. Or by assuming something was safe and innocent when it was not. I saw hollow power poles in a small town have a devastating effect. A lot of explosives can be hidden in a pole. And the concrete pieces become lethal.'

Halim mused aloud. 'A power pole in Baghdad?'

'Could you guarantee you were only going to hit the Americans? A blast from something like that will kill many believers also. You do not want their blood on your hands.'

'You are very right about that.'

His voice carried no conviction. He was, after all, only one cog in a bigger, invisible machine neither of us could really see, and which was driving him as much as it was driving me. That machine had made it clear we were fighting the Americans. It was the war I had fought many years earlier in 1991 and witnessed more recently. Now it was a war by another means. My staff college lecturer would like the sound of Clausewitz bastardised in this way.

'We will test in a way that you suggest. You will be witness to the test again. We will let you know when.'

11

Malik

I am a very happy man in these days. These days are like a new life is starting and I am full of hope. Hope can make even the hard things an easy yoke on the heart. Many things give me hope. My family, of course. But the changes at the shop amaze me. I have made a new friend in the young man who is working in his new job in the Foreign Ministry. I am a happy man because there are shirts being sold. That is not everything a man should have. Money helps. But a good friend. Good children. A good wife. A happy house. A flat roof under a velvet-blue night sky and a cream-yellow moon. These are things that make a man content. And good conversation that calms the heart.

Let me tell you about the new friend. He has an old name but I like it. Tawfik. It means to make oneself right with your friend. With God. With your neighbour. To have no bitterness towards another because you have reconciled with those you were tempted to hate. I told

Tawfik I liked his name very much because of these meanings. He was respectful to me but he demurred.

'Mr Malik,' he responded, acknowledging my seniority (I am a young old man!), 'this name was given me by my parents. I do not know what it really means and have never considered it. And I can be very sure my parents were not thinking about these ideas when they gave me this name.'

'Ah, that might be so but there are unspoken reasons for you to be given a name. Maybe its meaning was being saved for these better days when you might be in a new job where you can bring old enemies to the talking table.'

'I have many years to go before I will be responsible for that sort of work. No one will be trusting me with anything except making the tea.'

'Tawfik, Tawfik, I doubt that very much. With your new shirts I think you will be in the Minister's office very quickly. I think he will want to see the nice shirts your friends are talking about. He will want to know where you bought them.'

'I will tell him the pigeon sellers at the Souk al-Ghazal had them flown in from Palestine!'

'Aha, I believe you would, I believe you would. But that is not the sort of talk I would expect from an educated man. Your father would be embarrassed at such mocking of a senior man.'

Tawfik laughs. 'My father is the source of such nonsense. I learn this talk from him.'

'He is still alive?'

'My father? Yes, he still lives.' Tawfik was reflective for a moment.

'And yet he has not married off such a handsome son?'

His black eyes danced in amusement. 'In these times you want to think of marriage? I fear that is not for me until we sort out this mess.'

'What is with you young people? My wife has a close relative. Very beautiful and a perfect wife for a man like you. But she thinks the same crazy thoughts as you. It is craziness, I tell you. In these terrible times you should be looking to create your own happiness.'

Tawfik's response was cut off by the tinkle of glassware in the doorway. Mahrus stood there with a tray of coffee glasses, his chin tilted in the direction of his shop.

I slap Tawfik's shoulder. 'Enough crazy talk, come and drink with Mahrus.'

Since Tawfik visited the first time he has come back several times bringing with him friends who wished also to buy the sharp-looking cotton shirts. For them I unlocked the trays of cufflinks which I had hidden away until a time such as this. Locked away for men who knew what they were buying and who would admire what they saw and what they wore.

After three Holy Days had passed, the young men began sitting with Mahrus and talking serious politics and world affairs. Mahrus was a surprise to them. He was a surprise to me too. I did not know he had travelled around the world as an official with the Ministry of Agriculture. He had views about how food was grown. He thought deeply about how it was bought and sold. And he knew the politics, the anger and hatred that came from fighting over that food. He told stories of ancient governments which had risen and fallen around the waters that flowed out of Turkey, across our deserts and into the Arabian Gulf. He told how the British and other powers had marked out the states around our water and oil. Water first. Always water. But grain. And spices. And trade routes. Stories and legends which shaped our world.

Mahrus provoked and argued and lectured these young men, who were now getting foreign-affairs lessons they were not expecting. Nor was I expecting the instruction. But I was attentive too. I listened because I was hearing a new man. It was as if another Mahrus had been unleashed and all it had taken was an audience which would engage his intellect. Who else, had they wandered these lanes, would have inclined to the wisdom of a shop owner? Yet here they came, sometimes walking the two kilometres or so from the Ministry after work, or occasionally tumbling out of an overloaded taxi in the middle of the day when they thought they could escape for an hour or so. I listened because I could see that this was the new Iraq, in which a man could speak freely on the street. But a man who was encouraged to do so because the young men hungered after it first. This was a new thing also.

The young men were talking to each other in front of the shop, sitting on those chairs I had borrowed, and on wooden crates and other props gathered for their growing number. Mahrus hung back in his doorway space. Some days he showed it was taking time for his cautious habits to die.

'Iraq can make its own way now without the Americans.' It was a common theme.

'But can we mend our country without them? Can we do what the South Africans did with the Truth and Reconciliation Commission? Will we need help for that? I think so.' That was not a common theme. I was startled.

'We need help with that sort of reconciliation but we do not need Americans. See how they are still divided with black and white, and Mexicans are the new black in America.'

'Hispanics.'

'What?'

'Mexicans. And others from Latin America from Iberian roots. These are the Hispanic people.'

'Big English words. They hurt my head.'

They all laughed and then Mahrus spoke gently into the quietness. 'No house can mend itself. Look at my shop. Its heart is good. There is good coffee here, no?'

'There is good coffee here, Mahrus.'

'But I need a man who can help with the tiles. And to mend the electricity. And someone to fix the refrigerated counters. And I need money. I cannot mend this house of mine. I need help. Just like we did in the 1950s when we needed help with our agriculture.'

'We needed help with our agriculture? This has always been the bread basket of the Middle East. How did we need help?'

'In those days we were not the bread basket. We were people out of the deserts and out of the towns and mountains. We could grow enough for each small tribe or town or village. But we could not feed ourselves or our neighbours. We grew up too dependent on buying what we needed.'

This was how it had started. Mahrus soon had their attention and a long coffee session began. And so it went for weeks. It continues even now. But in the beginning it was special, for there was a new tone in Mahrus. It sounded like hope. There was hope in me. There was so much hope I closed the shop for a short hour one afternoon and walked into the lanes along the river looking for a man who repaired glass. He asked if his brother could repair the stone around the front of the shop; his brother needed work. I said he could bring his brother if it was the sort of stone he could repair. The next day there was still so much hope in my heart that had not faded away into the darkness I went to the bazaar and bought a tin of paint. It was white paint. It had no paper wrapper but a serial number stencilled on its silver side. It had '-00-' in the stock number so I knew it had come from American stores somewhere. That was okay by me. This was an American way to help our country. I imagined the stall owner had somehow blessed his family, thanks to this stolen paint.

On the afternoon of the Friday, when Mahrus was at prayers, the two brothers came and measured each store. That night the stonemason came back with many of his friends and they removed the cracked and broken stone and cemented new stone in place. They said they would return later and finish the grout, when the cement under the stone had set properly. The next morning I arrived at the shop to see Mahrus sitting in front of his store with a coffee in his hand. He was by himself. It was the first time in many years I had arrived to see him sitting, not standing. For the first time in years he did not look like he was getting ready to run.

'There are angels, Malik. But these ones work at night.' He sat with his back to the shops so he could watch the street. It was a new relaxed and cheerful Mahrus.

'There are angels, Mahrus,' I agreed. 'There are angels. Some of them will be here soon and they are bringing glass for this shop. They will make a difference to the work I have to do here. Maybe we can get a generator next for both shops. We can stay open a little longer each day. Maybe install some lights in our shops.'

He looked at me for a moment. There was no expression. Then he smiled a faint smile. 'Lights? Ha, I would like a heater for those winter days. Those gas heaters I have make things humid and the pastries go soft. And how about some cooling at this time of the year? Maybe some fans again.'

'We can do those things. All those things, Mahrus, as the money comes in. I feel things are getting better.'

'I truly hope so. But look out. Here come those boys. It must be Saturday. They have no work at the office but have come here to learn the ways of the world.'

'You like them, I can see.'

He looked up from his coffee. 'Just don't tell them, eh.'

I am restless on the rooftop this evening. I have not seen or heard helicopters for many days but there are shadows tonight. Silent devils. I can see the slowly falling stars as they glare at the ground and look for their prey, seeking the mice of men scurrying among the lanes of Baghdad. Maybe bad mice, but the signs in the sky are not good. My unease is not helped by two young people with so much reason to hope, but who cannot bring themselves to dream. I am consoled just a little that Tawfik was not offended by my clumsy words about marriage, though when the boys left our street Mahrus chastised me for being so forward. Saleema just smiles and asks me not to push Fatimah.

She comes over and takes my arm and tells me to stop fretting. My shirt is hanging over the back of the chair, hidden in the dark near the wall. The night is hot and my skin slick with sweat. I have not been doing hard work. It is just very hot. And I am worried about the omens.

'You told me Mahrus thought there was something wrong the other day at the shop,' she says softly. 'But nothing happened. You were delighted.'

I nod. She is right. How long after the bombs and the shootings stop do we become less alert? When do we stop seeing omens and signs and warnings in things not sent from God? What if we never stop seeing them? Will part of me be dead still then? I think of Mahrus and know his smile is a better smile for the young men who now drink his coffee and sit at his feet. That which was dead is alive again, even though he is still poor. We will live again. The flares drop away to the east in a silent, slow shower of light and I think of other signs from the east. There are words in the Book that come to my mind.

To God belongs the East and the West;
Wherever you turn to, there is the Face of God;
God is all-embracing, all-knowing.

That is all I need tonight to put my fears to rest. Tomorrow I will see what the sun will bring. I embrace Saleema and we go down the stairs into the hot dimness of the house.

12

Aadil

Ha, you are back again with your notebook. No camera yet? These yellow and green bruises are not as pretty as when they were blue and black, are they? They hint too much at something rotting. You shake your head. I wonder. The engineer's story still enchants you? You are a strange person, indeed. Do you have the newspapers I asked for? No?

How do you expect me to continue my story if there is nothing in return? Any news of my family, perhaps?

Promise me you will get news of my family and I will tell you how the second test of my triggers was a stupid and insane test and nearly got me killed. Promise? On whose honour? What do you mean, 'Your parents!' Truly you confirm for me what Allah knows already – that you have no honour.

That is enough. No arguments. I have no appetite for arguments. Sit still and I will talk.

The second test came about in unsettling circumstances. Have I mentioned it almost got me killed? I think I did. Forgive me. Being strung up like a dog in this cell day after day plays tricks with my mind. I cannot remember if I have said something or if it has wafted past in a vapour of a dream. Hmm, let's see. The circumstances of the second test … Because of the location of the first test I worried this one could injure and maybe even kill believers. It was unsettling because I was not able to see or contact or know those who were conducting it. I was nervous because I knew I could be implicated by my presence. I knew those unseen people who paid me wanted me to know that if I betrayed them my life was in their hands. It is not a good sensation to not be trusted. An officer can always be trusted.

The highway through the part of the city where the test occurred was broad. There were three lanes of traffic in each direction, and businesses lined each side of the street. Many of the buildings were permanently closed, though some were being refurbished and others being rebuilt. Many had been shattered in the fighting of 2003 and only now were people brave enough to reopen them. Private contracting companies working for the American administration had dug and installed new power and phone connections. It was the phone connections that had been targeted by Halim and his friends.

I was to visit a store that imported bolts of cloth and distributed them to garment makers in the city. It was cheap cloth, but as I pulled up near the address I had been given I saw lots of different shops with all manner of cloth in their windows. The street had an unfamiliar air about it, as if it was new and re-energised. There was new glass in the windows. The pavements were dusty but the rubbish had been swept into piles, as if awaiting a regular garbage service. Palms had been planted, young and fragile in this heat and tied up with hessian, feet damp from regular watering. This part of the city was looking prosperous; its citizens dared to think they could return to a regular trading life. I was a little startled at the new construction, the smell of paint, the still-green concrete paths not yet cured, and the signs of builder's rubble everywhere. And, as always, I was worried about the glass. No, that is not true. I was terrified of the glass. Have you seen glass wounds? You cannot see the shards in the body among all the blood. You cannot even see them under an X-ray. People can die from airborne glass. But people die slowly from the inside out from glass bullets too. I hate the glass. I knew if there was going to be a large explosion here, there was every chance all that glass in the refurbished shopfronts would be lethal.

Despite my fear I stopped and looked in the window of the shop I was about to enter. The mannequins were nothing like what I had ever seen in Iraq. They were colourful, with large, mournful, painted eyes and short, buzz-cropped hair. They stood there alone, waiting to be dressed, and crowded me with images of neon-lit shops in Berlin.

I walked into the store and asked for Hussein. I did not know Hussein but Halim had insisted I ask for him.

A man about my age came from out of the back of the store. I guessed he was once a military man as well. I asked where he had served. His dark bushy eyebrows lifted in surprise.

'You think I was in the military?'

'It is hard to take the military out of a person. Too much is drilled into a man in all those years on the parade ground.'

He shook my hand with a firm grip but showed no interest, nor did he reply directly to my query. 'There is much more for us to be concerned about now than to be thinking about yesterday. But I have some experience in the things we are doing today that I hope will keep me and my family safe. And perhaps we will see the Americans driven from this Holy Land. Come, I want to show you something.'

I followed him out through the back of the shop. I was on edge. I did not know this man. Perhaps he was my executioner. They could copy the original triggers I had built for them and now dispose of me. I reassured myself that they did not have the more sophisticated trigger yet. Perhaps that would keep me safe. I did not know. All I could do was obey and follow. I could not stop. I followed the broad back and shuffling walk of this Mr Hussein, my age and not admitting to military life. I wondered if he was in one of the security services. Men who had about them an air of military discipline and order, and who declined to own any military allegiance to regiments, brigades or divisions, who had no units or badges with which they could share a fraternity, were usually from the security services. A man who was a regular soldier would admit his units in a heartbeat. Sometimes men of the security services were rejected by the regular soldier, who was often frightened by them, and who might express his fear in derision and dismissal.

My head was full of these thoughts as I followed Mr Hussein down the lane behind the shops and into a new concrete-block building being decorated with its first coats of paint. There were wires hanging from the ceiling and out of the walls. The doors and windows were still to be fitted. Dust lay thick on the floor. A number of tradesmen were mixing plaster and others were preparing paint. We left them and climbed the stairs to a large room on the second floor where two empty fuel drums supported a plank. Three young men with fierce eyes looked me over as I walked in. Clearly they were a team and I was an intruder. Their mouths were shut but their eyes told me I was not welcome. There were no introductions and I was motioned to sit down. No names were exchanged. No greetings. We were about three hundred metres further down from where I had parked, which turned out to be a fortunate distance, as events would prove. From this shell of a room I could see up and down the street. Cars and SUVs crept along the highway. With a roadblock manned by the Americans half a kilometre away, drivers knew that approaching these checkpoints at anything other than a crawl could be lethal.

When I reflect on what happened that afternoon I think we made two mistakes. In the first place we were sitting in the middle of the target area. What was this whole team doing so close to an American roadblock? And on top of that our behaviour was suspicious. There we were, in full view of any who happened to look our way. Sitting side by side on a bench. In an empty room. Doing nothing. Not even talking. How many men sit like that and never talk to each other? We should have been painting or working on the building, not looking like spectators. We looked exactly like what we were – an audience waiting for the curtain to rise, a game to start, something to happen. To any covert teams out there observing, we would have stood out plainly. I sweat when I think how foolish we were.

The whine of the engine of the Abrams tank is very distinctive. It is a powerful sound and echoes off the buildings and the hard hot air of the desert, so you cannot always tell where the tank is coming from. I could hear it but I could not see it. As the whine got louder I thought there were two, maybe three of them. After a short time two tanks came into view from the south, travelling past the empty window space from my left and grinding up the highway towards the checkpoint. Behind them some armoured personnel carriers, then a large number of semitrailer trucks, most carrying twenty- or forty-foot shipping containers. Without any warning a modest flash and a dull thump saw the fifth truck in the column on its side, sliding across the highway, the container pierced, and the truck bursting fiercely into flames. Black smoke smothered the boiling ulcer of fire, which rapidly enveloped the vehicle and the one following it, though this truck continued to speed through and emerged from the pall. The convoy was well disciplined, for all the vehicles sped up and continued forwards. None stopped.

It was not the convoy that shocked me but what happened even before the truck stopped sliding across the highway. With a shout and a leap, his phone in his hand, Mr Hussein jumped into the air and waved wildly. He danced a short dance with a grin on his face then dropped to the floor in a heavy thud as his chest opened for just a brief moment, though in the movie of my mind it seems to be open forever. Then it closed as quickly and concrete blocks behind him shattered into hundreds of fragments. His blood was spattered across the floor and walls in the blink of an eye. I did not wait to see what would happen next, for in a heartbeat I knew that what I had been warning Halim about had come to pass. We were being watched. From a long distance. By a sniper team which had no doubt wondered at our strange behaviour. Confirmed perhaps by Mr Hussein and his suspicious phone and triumphant dance.

As his body folded to the floor in a shower of blood and dust and paint flakes, I fell sideways off the bench and crawled to where he lay, retrieved his phone and searched for a way out. Already I could hear the sound of helicopters. I rolled over to see where my companions were. One was already missing his head, his torso lying back against the newly damaged wall, as if he were taking a workman's short break. I was shocked. That might have been me. Or any one of us. The other two men ran for the door. But running was not the answer. Whatever the sniper team was using, it was of an extreme calibre, big enough to remove a head, and fired from so far away we did not hear the shot. My only chance to escape with my life was to join the tradesmen below, who would be evacuating the building and scrambling for their vehicles and away from the uproar.

I rolled to the top of the stairs, gathered myself to a crouch, then leaped and tumbled down to the lower floor, hoping to the pit of my stomach I was not visible through any of the windows. Another of the upstairs crew fell through the stairwell, his leg gone from the pelvis down. Blood sprayed against the wall and mixed pink and crimson in the plaster and paint dust. I could only guess that he had paused to see what was going on. He lay there and watched his life pour out, not fighting the inevitable. He died without a sigh or word. His blood just stopped and his eyes remained fixed on the hole through which he had fallen.

I snatched up a wire-handled plastic bucket with wet remnants of plaster in it, grabbed a trowel and smeared plaster on my clothes, then flicked more onto my hair and hands. The six or seven painters and plasterers gathered on the bottom floor stood anxiously eyeing their trucks. The question hung in the air: would we be shot at if we tried to drive away? Everyone paused for a second or two in the doorway then ran for a vehicle, stumbling over tiles and rubble and slipping in mortar sand scattered around the site. I followed some men onto the tray of a truck and relaxed slightly when I realised we were most likely protected from a shooter thanks to a brick wall that surrounded the house block. As I seated myself in the truck, my hands worked quickly to extract the SIM card from Mr Hussein's phone and place it in my mouth. I shoved the phone into the plaster where it was barely hidden. It would be ruined in the wet mix but all I cared about was that it should not be found. He was a fool to dance like that. Maybe he was a fool to store numbers on the phone instead of the SIM. I was taking no chances and chewed the card as best I could. I would spit the pieces out later.

I don't know what the others on the truck thought of my presence. No one spoke. They were shocked and fearful. No one wanted to know anything that could get them into trouble, I suppose. Or maybe they were not innocent either, such is the soul of this place.

My heart hammered in my throat as the truck lurched into the back lane and away from the awful carnage we had just witnessed. Three helicopters circled overhead. How did they get there so quickly? Did the others know as I did that those helicopters would be watching every move, ready to pounce in a heartbeat? There would be more aircraft we could not hear or see, and I knew I needed to behave with care. With innocence.

We had barely got going up the laneway when we came up short against an American patrol of Humvees travelling towards us. I could feel each man freeze against the side of the truck as the soldiers roared at us and gestured at us to dismount. Slowly we shuffled off and each man was patted down, the soldiers shouting, angry and nervous, all hiding their fear behind their sunglasses but letting it out in their voices and their strutting, even slapping us in their frustration. Their sergeants called them into line but with little conviction.

The Americans, alert and agitated, peered in my plaster bucket, and patted me down for weapons. Finding nothing on any of us they growled and waved us back on board. The truck took off and I vowed to never get in this position again. These men I worked for were amateurs. I was lucky to be alive. I was lucky to be free and alive, and a rapid survey of my fellows told me they knew the same. The hands of the man opposite me shook so much he clutched them under his armpits. No one spoke.

I jumped off when two men were dropped off a few suburbs away and walked on without looking back. Once out of sight I retrieved the phone from the thickening plaster, dropped the bucket on a pile of street rubbish, and caught a taxi home.

But it was not over yet. I had to extricate my car from in front of Mr Hussein's store. Would that prove to be a fatal mistake? People in the store had seen me leave with Mr Hussein but neither of us come back. Then they would see that my vehicle was gone. Would they ask if I was connected with the blast? If Mr Hussein was connected?

Yet I could hardly leave my car in the vicinity of the explosion, could I? People can, and do, make the right connections for the wrong reasons. It was a risk, but after cleaning up and changing my clothes, I caught a bus back to the area. My car sat parked where I had left it. Would anybody be watching it? Would anyone associate it with the earlier explosion? I could not know. One thing was for certain – the longer I left it there the likelier it was that someone would ask awkward questions. I climbed in and drove away. As I did so, one small consolation arose in my mind. I knew my device was functional and that this crew worked their explosives well, planning shaped charges that could be set into the phone junction boxes and knock over a heavy vehicle. Would it work on a tank or an armoured personnel carrier? I did not know and after that day I did not care to know.

13

Malik

My name is Malik. I live in Baghdad and I still drive to work every day past a big American roadblock with crouching Abrams tanks, a forest of gun barrels and nervous soldiers. I remain careful. Now, when I come off the bridge, if I look over to the left I get a glimpse of our two shops. It is a very brief snapshot but I tell you that it makes me glad to be in Baghdad. I am better than when I started to tell you this story. Then, I was coming to the shop in hope that one day there would be hope. I wanted things to improve. But I was down to my very last hope. Only the prayers on the rooftop each night sustained me. How to keep a family in food when there were no customers? How to keep Imaad in school when there were no customers? If I stayed on the rooftop I might have jumped off in craziness. But there are some things believers should not do, so I go to the shop instead. And now I think God has answered a prayer.

Mahrus jokes about the unseen angels. He waves at the tobacco remains scattered on the ground. 'Those angels smoked filthy cigarettes.'

'Oh?'

'Uh-huh.'

'Camels?'

'No, something they grew themselves, I think.'

'But did they do a good job with the stones?'

'It is a job sent from heaven. I see they came and put in some glass as well.'

As I unlock the security grille for the day I admire the glass. This time there are no big pieces of plate glass. Instead this is more expensive safety glass set in many wooden frames to make each piece smaller. The glass man said this is best in case there are bombs. It seems a good idea to plan like this when man-made yellow-and-blue tinted stars still fall from the night sky.

'But there are no angels who paint, Mahrus. Maybe that is a job for devils only.' I hold up the tin of paint and wave it towards him and he laughs at me. 'I think we wait to see the painting before we say if it is by angels or devils.'

'Yes, yes, I think we know before I open this tin of paint that it will be a devil painting.'

But truly I am a good painter. I know I should not praise myself but I do have a good eye and a steady hand and I like making the paint flow from the brush. It is a good thing to see old things made new and fresh again.

I start by clearing all the shirts from the shop window area. They will stay in their plastic for some months yet.

I think it will be a sign our future is secure when the shirts are all stacked on shelves and there is no plastic except in the basement. I wipe all the wood then paint around the windows and the frames. The man from the electronics store pauses on his way to work and gives me some advice. I do not stop to listen. I am not rude. I want to paint outside before the wind starts to blow the dust and sand. And I want to paint before the cool sun of the morning becomes the oven of midday. When it becomes the oven it will shine onto Mahrus's shop and he will lower a tattered canvas awning. He told me he bought it in Beirut many years ago. It is in sad shape now and he has stitched many pieces of fabric to it to hold it together. The electronics man wanders off to buy coffee from Mahrus, but his place is taken by two others who stop and become my instructors, who know everything about painting, drink their coffee and give advice but do not offer to lift a brush. You might think this is a rude thing for them to do but it is not. They are simply helping in their own way. These visitors are signs the street is returning to how it should be. Not so long ago these men, if they were in the street at all, would not stop to talk.

Soon the outside is done and I move inside to paint. The men stay and talk to each other but with the glass now in the windows I cannot hear them. I cannot hear the cars as much anymore. That is very exciting for me. Now I feel like I am in my own premises again. I am no longer out on the street like a stall man or street vendor selling cheap watches from Kuwait. This is my own store and I feel proud. I will wash the floors and see if I can get the scent of timber to come back into the shop. I will wash the walls down too, and paint the ceiling. I had better paint the ceiling first. Then I look at all the shirts lying around and decide the ceiling can wait. I will put the fans on and get some music playing in here. And there should be a proper mirror on the wall. In a frame. This store is not in a bazaar, after all. It is a proper store. A respectable store.

When I drive into the courtyard this evening, my hands and hair are covered in drops of paint. My son laughs and tells me I am an old man. Then he is serious.

'Baba, I want you to come to school tomorrow. We have a science day. We have all the fathers coming.'

'Tomorrow? Boy, I am working in the shop. How can I come to school?'

'I am sorry, Baba. Another day maybe.'

'Maybe another day.' He is disappointed. I see it in his face. But a day away from the shop is a day when maybe we do not have enough to eat. He walks off and picks up his blue school satchel. It has a cartoon of a strange yellow-haired boy on it. My son likes it. It is an American cartoon. He says he has seen it on a DVD at a friend's house. I have not seen it but it was the bag Imaad chose. He walks inside and I follow, after making sure the gates to the street are locked. My wife sees me and scolds me with her eyes. Then with her mouth.

'You are happy, no?'

'Yes. You know. You do not have to ask.'

'If you are happy why do you make your son sad?'

'I cannot leave the shop.'

She rolls her eyes at the roof. I do not like that habit of hers. It is like my mother and she makes a strange sound with her lips like my mother does.

'Pfffftt. You went to the shop when there was no one to buy your goods. How little a thing it would be now when there are people buying. You will be at the school for an hour. Maybe not even that long.'

More than the rolling of her black eyes, I hate it when she makes sense. I nod and say nothing but go to my son's room where he is taking books out of his bag.

'Take me to school tomorrow. I need to learn something.' He laughs because he thinks I am making a joke. But I am not. I still need to learn something about getting back to normal.

My son is very happy to be driving to school in the car. In the morning we make good time and arrive early. There are some builders working on repairing gaps in the school wall. My son moans about that. 'We have to go the long way.'

'But it is safer.'

'Baba, we are only safer from girls throwing sand at us. Anything else, even this old car, could drive through that wall.' I look at him in surprise. He is thinking and talking like a boy older than he is. Perhaps I have missed something in his growing up. I pat his head and say, 'I hope not.'

We walk to the front gate where there are men who were never at my school when I was a boy. Men with rifles. Men checking the bags of the children. Cars cannot get too close to the front gate. Even our schools have to be careful. This is a sad thing. But my boy has known only this and thinks it is the usual routine. He has his bag open and ready and the guard does not inspect too closely as we push through. I am walking with many other men. We look nervous and some are shy. I feel shy. I do not know why, but I am a mixture of shyness and pride. And when I examine close inside myself I know I am very happy my son is going to school. Here he will learn that boys from all backgrounds have the same dreams about work and play and meeting a nice girl and having a happy family. It does not matter if you are a Sunni. Or a Shia. My Kurdish friends have the same dreams. Sometimes I think of the men in the trenches of Iran who shot at us. They were bad shots. So were we. We were too nervous and scared to shoot straight. They were men who had dreams of peace, too, of families, of growing old and of picnics by the river.

I follow the fathers along the corridors and we find our way to the different classrooms. The men are all dressed in simple clothes and I see some who are in sandals and old torn trousers. They are struggling to live. In winter it will be much more difficult. How to get wood or coal or gas to cook and keep warm? If a man does not have a job, his family might help out, providing income which is small and may seem insignificant, but which ensures their survival. Running errands, selling trinkets in a small stall, scrounging scrap metal, doing anything that will earn payment. But if the family cannot find even this sort of work, I wonder how they live. Some I know from my mosque. Others I think I know from army days but I am not sure. We were boys then. Now beards and stubble and age and sun and tiredness cover our faces. We all mirror the lives we have lived. These men are weary and torn. But today these men also shine a little.

Our boys are at their benches and we are crowded around the walls. I notice the new paint. And the pictures. A skeleton with missing ribs and two black eyes, painted by the boys maybe, in the corner. Maps of the world on the walls. Charts and tables and graphs pinned up with precision, some obviously drawn by the boys, some by the teacher. Many are prints from magazines. There are few materials but the teacher is making an effort. The room looks like a real classroom. I understand why my son likes being here. I like being here. Saleema was right, this is what I had to do.

The boys stand suddenly when a tall and commanding man with black eyes, heavy eyebrows, square shoulders and strong forearms walks out of a small room adjoining the classroom. He nods to the boys and smiles in welcome.

'*Assalamu alaikum.*'

'*Wa alaikum assalaam.*'

The boys sit down in a clatter of steel-framed chairs.

'Welcome to our science class. My name is Aadil Hassan.' He speaks directly and firmly like many officers who led me. I hold my breath.

'We are going to show you the things we have been doing in class. This will be strange to many of you. Your own classrooms were not a place where your parents came. But this is an opportunity for you to see how clever your children are. And you will also see how important it is that even though we live in hard times we teach our children good lessons so they can help build this country again. That is not a task for Americans or British or Frenchmen or Germans. That is a task for Iraqis. And if we do not teach them constructive things here in the class they will only learn to fight in the streets with guns and bombs. These are not skills we want loose out there.'

A few men nod. I nod. This is sensible talk. Many men give no response. We have grown up in a country where it was dangerous to agree or disagree with what was being said. You could never tell if the response you chose would get you into trouble with the secret police. So the men standing around the room mainly watch and listen and remain mute, attending Mr Aadil like hawks.

He has a strong air of authority. He is not someone I would want to argue with. He sees everything and everyone and maybe even can see what we are thinking. Men like that in the army were people we followed into the trenches of Iran. But there were too few like this, with fire in their eyes, command on their lips and conviction in their voices. This man was maybe a senior officer.

For the next two hours the boys stand and explain different experiments of physics, chemistry and biology. They tell us about how metal is made, what the tensile strength of concrete means, and how flowers are pollinated. They illustrate with pictures they have drawn themselves. If one of the students stumbles or forgets some information, Mr Aadil gently prompts him and the boy soon gets back on track. Even the shyest boys stand up and are encouraged by Mr Aadil. I am very happy with this man and the work the boys have done. I have so much to tell Mahrus. And then I am the proudest father there, for Mr Aadil calls my boy to stand up and present his project.

Imaad rises to his feet and pulls from his bag a shoebox that has some corners bent. I have not seen the shoebox before. The guard has not seen it either, I think. Imaad glances at me before speaking to Mr Aadil. He is embarrassed. Did I smile for him? I hope I did but I am worried that I look anxious and unnerve him. So I try to keep my face straight while he talks.

He speaks about how a bird flies. He demonstrates with a feather and then with a model wing how a bird can climb into the air. He shows the hollow bones. He tells us how a bird can steer through the air with its bent feathers and by using its tail. I am bursting with pride and when he finishes I clap my hands. No other father has clapped his hands. My boy turns red in the face as he sits down. Some of the other men laugh and clap too. Mr Aadil thanks my boy and then thanks us for clapping. The next boys all get applause from the fathers too, so at the end Mr Aadil asks the boys who spoke first to stand up and we all clap them. I am glad we do. It pleases the boys. Mr Aadil is a clever man. He knows how to make students work at school. He knows what interests them. And he knows that if we praise each other we can help each other do great things. Even our children can be praised.

When the lesson is finished the fathers start to leave the classroom. We are silent but I can see boys turning to find their fathers or uncles or grandfathers, waving and smiling at them. The fathers wave back. I go to Mr Aadil and shake his hand. A traditional kiss does not seem right with this formidable man. But I want to give him respect. 'Mr Aadil, what you do here is a good thing,' I say. 'My boy wants to learn and to come to your class. I thank you for putting this spark of learning in him.'

Mr Aadil takes my hand and his dark eyes do not leave mine. They are deep and convey many and mixed things. They are eyes haunted by his life. I can see that. There is something sad in there. He looks at me very hard but his voice is soft, not like what I expect from a senior officer in the army.

'Thank you for your attendance today. I know the boys were excited about the lessons they would give their fathers. Your boy is a clever student. If he stays in class he will do very well. I think one day he will go to university.'

'*Shukran.*' Thank you. We finish shaking hands and I leave the classroom. There are no guards on the gates when I leave to drive to the shop. It is going to be a good day and my heart is very light. To university. If only my father were alive to hear that.

14

Aadil

I see you are quiet today. You think I will be angry perhaps? You do not want to tell me bad news about not contacting my family? Aha, your eyes betray you. No news. But you have a newspaper, I see. Perhaps you can ask the guard when I will be let out of these shackles? In lieu of finding my family. But you cannot give up trying to find my family, you understand? Or is it that you can now see an engineer might have a story after all? I do, I do.

They wanted a new test. The earlier one was not sufficient. Halim appeared without warning.

'We are ready for your next test.'

'You might be. I am not.'

'The devices are not ready?'

Halim was not to be swayed. He stood and slapped his hand on the table in frustration. 'You need to understand, we have a timetable we are working to. These tests need to be held and held soon. They cannot wait. Get the devices to me immediately,' he hissed as he straightened up and walked out, leaving me once again to pay for the food and coffee.

The transmitter and the receiver device had actually been ready for some weeks but I did not want to be pressed. In fact, I was planning a low-level function test at the Allawi al-Hilla bus station quite soon. Why there? I needed to test in a place with lots of people, just in case something went wrong. Hiding in a crowd is the best way. But the Allawi al-Hilla bus station is also a very dangerous place, with many American tanks and armoured personnel carriers and troops on patrol. There were some bad bombings there last year and security is tight. It is also close to the International Zone, where many foreigners work. So my guess was there would be in place many electronic countermeasures designed to stop the sort of transmission I wanted to send. If I could make the devices work at the Allawi al-Hilla bus station I was convinced I could make them work anywhere.

It was a simple test and one that pleased me. I purchased two radios with CD players in them. Each had an aerial which helped with my design. Inside one player I placed the transmitter. It was a difficult thing to do, but I took all the parts out and repackaged the radio in its carton, leaving the box open at the top just enough so that I could press the PLAY button. That would activate the transmitter for one-quarter of a second only. Even that was too long. But one-quarter of a second was what

I needed to get my instructions into the air and floating over to the receiver. It was enough time to send the signal many times in case there was interference. I also wired up a smaller radio inside the transmitter so that if it was tested by any guard or soldier they would hear a local radio station play. I had to hope they would not want to test the CD, since I had to remove the CD parts to install my transmitter. You will hear I had good reason to be glad that I had taken that precaution.

In the receiver I placed a small board of my own design and making. It was good work and I was very pleased with the results. This small board detected the signal and interpreted it so that a tiny relay was activated and the real radio receiver was switched on when it received the command from the transmitter. So my test was simple. I had the radio transmitter with me and my boy – no, you do not need to know his name – would have the receiver sitting beside him on the other side of the bus terminal compound. If I pushed the PLAY button and the other radio started playing a local radio station, I knew my design worked. Unlike my idiotic employers, I did not need to test with explosives.

It was a simple plan but what I could not know was what might happen when those signals were loose in the air. Would the Americans catch them and respond with automatic fire, shooting at the source without worrying who was there? Or would they respond and hunt us down? Or would they detect the signals and not know where they originated? Or would we elude them altogether? I hoped for the latter, and prayed for none of the former. I was counting on the crowds to protect us.

On a busy Saturday afternoon I went with one of my boys to the Allawi al-Hilla bus station. He carried the receiver in his backpack. I told him I wanted to return the player and some other electronics from the school to the store where I had bought them. But first I was to meet a friend off the bus from Fallujah. It was a good lie and easily supported with some spare parts from the classroom, which I could explain. I did not tell him I had a radio and CD player in my briefcase, along with some school papers from the boys, an apple and some pens and pencils.

We arrived at the station, shuffled through the crowded checkpoint and had our bags searched. We talked as we walked through and there was nothing amiss. The guards looked in each of our bags and no questions were asked of my son. One of them thought the childish drawings in my own bag unusual, but when I explained I was a teacher he waved me through.

We waited a while and saw numerous buses come and go. I wandered over to the timetable board many times and asked about buses from Fallujah. After we waited two hours and I had shown plenty of frustration I left my son sitting on a bench at the side of the compound. I walked to the timetable again, gazed at it, took out the apple and as I did so pressed the PLAY button.

There was no immediate reaction from the Americans, but one came soon enough. I walked back to where my son was sitting. He had opened his bag and was peering inside, clearly perplexed.

'What is wrong?'

'Music is coming from my bag. But I didn't turn anything on.'

'I told you that radio had to be sent back.'

I tried to sound nonchalant but was not very convincing. My son caught the tone and stared at me still more puzzled.

'How could it turn on by itself?'

'Electronics can do random things. All the time. Let's turn it off and go to the shop before it closes and see if we can get it replaced.'

'But what about our visitor?'

'Ah, he must have been delayed. I will call him later and see what has happened. Come on. Let's get going.'

My son started to pull the carton from his bag to turn off the music. It was at that point I noticed the disturbance in the crowd. The bus station is an open place under a blue painted tin roof. Despite the large crowds, it is easy for the military to drive vehicles in there. The crowd was parting, but not willingly. They were shouting at an American armoured personnel carrier that was nosing towards us, preceded by three soldiers, alert and scanning the crowds. The carrier was bristling with aerials and its turret was traversing a small arc that covered the area where we stood. I guessed the very tiny signal had been detected. Fortunately the crowds had protected us and they had not simply fired at the signal source.

Success in two areas then. The signal had got through and had not been jammed. And so far I had not got my son killed. Or worse, badly injured. It was a good test. But we had to get safely away from there before I could claim total success. I took another bite of my apple as the soldiers approached. No matter what happened next we had to keep calm and I had to behave as an innocent passenger might behave.

'Hey, you there. What's that you're holding?'

Still chewing the apple I turned to see a soldier pointing a rifle at my son and another behind him screaming the question. My son was composed but he was still perplexed.

'It is a radio. We are returning it to the shop,' said my son. 'It keeps turning on by itself.'

'Keep your hands on the bench and slide away from the box.'

My gut churned as my boy looked towards me, but I maintained an encouraging voice and told him to do as the soldier said. 'You know it's a radio, but they don't. Just slide away a little so they can see.'

I then spoke to the soldier to let him know what my son was doing. There was the barest flicker of acknowledgement.

My son had not yet completely unpackaged the radio. The soldier motioned to him to lift the box flap and to put the radio on the ground. I told my son calmly what to do. The crowd had fallen back and was watching with curiosity. Some had burrowed well away, in case it was a bomb. But even in our maddest of days it would be unusual for a father and young son to suicide together. Yes, I know it has happened, but I think the soldiers – everyone – wanted to believe that even in our sunken city such things were truly uncommon. I think the soldiers believed that or they would have treated us more harshly.

The soldier giving instructions to my son stepped back and told him to turn the radio off. He obeyed, his hands moving like slow-shifting oil across concrete. Not too fast, not too slow. We have learned the correct response time in front of these nervous soldiers.

'Turn it on again.'

My son complied.

'Okay, turn it off.' The soldier shrugged and looked back at his sergeant standing beside the armoured personnel carrier. He shrugged in return. They said nothing but backed away, scanning the rest of the market and forgetting we even existed. As the diesel exhaust huffed into the air and the armoured beast retreated, the crowd swirled around and soon the terminal was swamped by fresh passengers. None paid us attention, but the sound of silent relief was audible to everyone. No one wanted a bomb, not even for the Americans. Not in this place anyway.

My son repackaged the radio and we walked out of the terminal, seeing the armoured personnel carrier losing its way, its cannon snout covering wider and more aimless arcs. It sensed something was wrong. It did not know exactly what it was. I was relieved but I was also aware of how dangerous were the components and devices I handled. They worked well. But they were to be used once and once only. Too much testing like this would soon have us found out.

With that successful test completed I was satisfied my designs worked, my construction of the boards was up to scratch and the disguise plausible. I thought through everything that might go wrong but could imagine no reason why Halim couldn't now have the first units. I gathered them up and visited the electronics shop. I handed them over with a packet of Winstons containing a note that read simply, 'Here they are.'

Saleh served up his coffee but I sensed his mood was not so courteous. Had I said something to offend him? Or maybe Halim had? Whatever the reason, his face wore a frown and the hospitality we were usually offered was absent. No matter, I would ask about that later. We waited until he had walked away to serve others before we spoke. Halim, too, was more wound up than usual. I was careful but I had to be blunt.

'The first six pairs of frequency-hopping devices are ready – I assume you have seen them. They are too dangerous to use in a test. They can be used only once. Do not test them. Just use them.'

'How do you know this? How can you be so sure?'

'I ran my own test and found myself looking up the wrong end of three rifles and a big cannon.'

'You ran your own test?'

'You should not act so surprised. These are dangerous devices and they will draw attention. And you can hardly blame me, given the results of the test supervised by your Mr Hussein, can you?'

He shook his head and said nothing, so I went on.

'I needed to run the test in an area where there would be excessive countermeasures. So I ran it close to the International Zone. The signal got through but it was detected and within a few minutes there was a patrol right on top of us.'

'Did they speak to you?'

'Not directly, but they spoke to my son.'

'Did they see or find anything?'

'They saw everything. Well, they saw the receiver housing at least. They saw it turned on and off and heard some beautiful Turkish music played over the radio. It sounded like Türkmenler.' I could not help but tease him. He was impatient, not amused.

'I do not understand.'

'I disguised the receiver as a radio. It plays a radio when I transmit. That was the test. Would the receiver turn on and the radio play? Simple really.'

He shook his head and gazed at the ground. I could see he was not pleased that I had exercised my own initiative. But he was determined to learn about the devices and quickly got refocused.

'So how do we use it?'

'In the packet of cigarettes here is a set of simple instructions. I have assumed that you want to disguise the devices in the same way as the one I tested. It's a good place to hide them and the radios are a handy power source. The instructions will tell you which wires to disconnect from the radio and which ones to connect to the detonator. You will always run the risk of having stray emissions trigger the detonator, but I have coded a sequence of signals before the device should blow. You need to push the PLAY button on the transmitter once. That will turn on the receiver. You then need to press the button a second time. That will send the coded signals to fire the detonator. You see, I have made it as safe as possible for you. But I have a word of warning.'

'What is that?'

'Never let the transmitter be found. You need to destroy it as soon as it has been used. Burning is best. Under an oxytorch. If it is found then there will be countermeasures put in place to stop them in the future. There will be a transmitter with every receiver and both need to be destroyed. If those chipsets are discovered, the Americans will quickly counter them and you will be back to square one.'

'I understand.'

'It is also best not to fiddle with that button, even out of idle interest. Pressing it will call in the Americans quicker than the Republican Guard did in Kuwait.'

He glared at me as he picked up the cigarette packet and dropped it in his jacket pocket. He had no sense of humour.

'So you will not do a test with us?'

It was my turn to stand in impatience and leave him with the bill. I slapped the table top.

'I will not. I have risked my life for you. And I risked the life of my son. I will never do that again. As I said, the devices are ready. They will work. Pick them up from the electronics store as I make them. Otherwise I do not think we have need of any more conversation. Good evening.'

15

Saleema

My name is Saleema. My husband is a proud man. He will not tell you he once had a large family of brothers who were very dear to him. They were killed in the war against Iran. He was in the war too and suffered some wounds. His flesh wounds healed but I do not think he has healed the wounds of his heart. He still feels sad for the family he lost. His war finished when a bunker fell on him. He told me once it was not hit by enemy fire but was badly built. They had been too hasty making the shelter. It fell down and many soldiers suffocated. Malik had a burned face and a broken back and spent a long time in a frontline hospital before he was properly mended. Now he hates being in the house or in any place which is closed up. He spends a lot of time on the roof. He does not always tell me what he is thinking up there. Sometimes confesses his mind goes back to the trenches and the bunkers of his brief time on the front, and how he hates this new fighting. He thought he had escaped the terror of war, but this new conflict brings to mind his dead brothers, and his father, who died of a broken heart in 1989.

It is not all darkness in his heart. He adores his children. We have a boy and two girls. He loves them all, but I know he looks on our son like he might have looked on his brothers. Sometimes he tells his children when they are sleeping that their uncles and their grandfather are angels looking over them. He does not think I can hear him. I hear his sadness. And his love.

He is a good son to his mother, as well. She lives with Malik's sister and her family in a suburb not far away. He has one other family relation he loves but has not seen in a long time. He is a cousin who left Baghdad with his family in 1991, when the city was on fire and the armies of our neighbours moved against us. They had an old car, which they drove through Baghdad in the middle of the night and through to Jordan. They took lots of soda bottles of petrol in the car to help them get there. They painted their car with a mixture of sand and mud, which dried hard in the sun. They did that to make it blend into the desert when they had to stop for rest. We all wonder at the brave foolishness of Malik's cousin. The American and British aircraft were flying unseen in the night and in the day, attacking vehicles on the roads. But somehow they made it to Jordan. Maybe a lone car travelling slowly up the highway was not worth a bomb or a missile. But they passed many trucks and military vehicles, whole convoys that were burned out and destroyed.

Yet here is a thing that puzzles Malik and is a source of anger for his cousin. He drove all that way with his family packed in that car painted with mud and everyone sitting next to all that fuel in small bottles. Can you imagine what would have happened if a plane had attacked them? They would have been incinerated. The cousin had preached his faith in the brotherhood of the Arab family. He thought he was safe from any infidel because in so many countries there was an Arab brother who would welcome him into his home and protect him. He said it was this bond that made the Arab family stronger than the family of Western nations. So he drove and drove on that hazardous road all the way to Jordan, expecting his Arab brothers would welcome him into the safety of their country. It was not unreasonable for him to think so, especially since his wife is a Jordanian citizen. So you can imagine his surprise and then his anger when he found himself parked in the desert on the Iraqi side of the border for the next two weeks, refused entry until the Jordanians saw which way the war was going. And even then it was not the Arab brotherhood who rescued him but his wife's family, who appealed to their government for help.

Malik is still convinced the Arab brotherhood is strong and that decent men will set the tone for our country again. The cousin is not convinced. He rages about how the Americans and British and Australians and Canadians flew their people out of Kuwait when there was trouble, but an Arab Jordan would not look after his wife and him and their family. He is very angry and disillusioned. He is so disillusioned with the Arab brotherhood he is now a British citizen.

They have never returned, you know. Many Iraqis live in countries surrounding Iraq. It might surprise you to know many even live in Iran. They are scared to return. They live close to the scent of Iraq, and the dust and the water and the soul of our civilisation. But they do not come home. One day maybe. Not yet. But this distant family is close to Malik's heart. They make him brave. He says if they can drive through the flames of hell with a car full of petrol and not die, then he can drive each day to the shop and be safe.

We are mostly lucky. Not every family has suffered wounding or killing. I do not know why that is. Just as there are those who do not know why they die, we do not know why we live. But we are glad we do and we do not take that for granted. We have not been very religious, but we observe our prayers and do not do any bad things. So maybe we are being smiled on by Allah Himself. But we are still very careful. And we are not entirely whole. Malik lost his brothers, and my own dear sister died with her family when their house collapsed on them in 1991. My beautiful niece Fatimah was left without her mother or father, her brothers or sister.

We do not talk about what happened to her parents, for that is a terror that only chokes us. Sometimes when Fatimah and I are at home together and trying on new clothes Malik has secretly imported for us, our giggling turns to tears. These days they are quiet tears but they are hot and fervent and we stop for a moment until the giggles return. When she smiles through those tears and tries to make me cheerful again, I can only hug her. She is my sister, after all. She will be a beautiful mother one day and bring joy to her own family. We chat when we are alone together, with Malik at his store and the children at play in front of the house, and we plan those happy days. We pray they are soon upon us, despite what Fatimah says to Malik about not wanting to invest in love in these violent times.

When Malik wanted to marry me and talked to my father, they spoke about honour. All men do is talk about honour. But then they spoke about living in a reputable and safe part of the city, and in the view of my father that could only be in the suburbs of Baghdad full of traders and merchants. For that is what my father was, a silk merchant. This is how Malik came to have a clothes shop. My father said merchants are peaceful, because they travel all over the country and around the world. Merchants meet foreign people in other countries and from those friendships come to learn that people everywhere share similar hopes and dreams. Malik likes that thought and wants to travel to see and hear this for himself. My father also says merchants are too busy making money to be violent. I do not know about that, you know. I have seen merchants arguing fiercely about prices. I think they can be violent sometimes. They are certainly very loud when they disagree.

I first met Malik when he was in a hospital where I worked in Fallujah. He was a good patient and I could see he was a thinker and a gentleman and very different from many of the military men who had shown interest in me. It is ironic to me that he was shaped so much by his experience in the army, even though he spent such a short time there. He wanted to go to university but the army took him before he finished his high school and when the army was finished with him he was broken. It took him some time to be mended. I think my father helped mend him when he loaned him money for a small stall. Malik was trying to sell shirts door to door, but it was a tough way to earn a living. So he started his stall. But there are thousands of shirt stalls. And all the shirts are the same. He asked my father how to make a better stall. My father used to say he felt sorry for Malik and could not afford to have a pauper hanging around, but I think the real reason he helped was that he recognised the trader in Malik. So he advised Malik that he needed to sell cheaper than his competition or find something unique to sell.

Then one day an old friend visited. He was still in the army but had been visiting Jordan and Lebanon. He wore a beautiful cotton shirt from Lebanon. That gave Malik an idea. He would sell only the best cotton shirts. Mainly white. There would be no polyester. It took a long time to build up the business but it was a good business and soon he had three stalls. Then he bought a store. It was a popular store because it was easy to get to from the city, where all the government people worked. Many who had worked overseas were pleased to get their shirts from him. Malik thought that business would be even better after 2003. But instead the situation did not improve. We thought the Americans would get rid of our dictator and then leave it to the Iraqis to set up a new government. Instead the Americans stayed and very soon so many old hatreds and feuds bubbled to the surface. Many were directed at the Americans and that is what the world thinks is going on. But we know here there is so much violence that is tribal. How many people think we are tribal? Yes, we still are and we solve things through tribal and old family allegiances, the roots of which none of us can ever hope to record, let alone remember.

For Malik and his store, the expectation that business would improve so quickly evaporated. It is hard to convince buyers to come to your shop when there are tanks shooting down the street where you are located. And if not tanks, there are armoured personnel carriers with their machine guns. And if not those weapons, there are Iraqis using the streets near the Tigris to shoot across the river at the Americans. So the Americans shoot back and patrol up and down, down and up, around and around. It is not an environment that encourages anyone to come and buy your goods.

We people of Baghdad will need to relearn how to be at ease, you know. We move from place to place far too directly. You understand, we only go to the street for very specific purposes and when we are done we return home.

To wander the street and gaze into windows, or to linger with friends and talk, is foreign to us, even though Malik tells me some young men now gather around Mahrus's shop for coffee. I do not say this to him but I worry about that. Who might see it and think they are a target worth attacking? I do not know. But I hide it from Malik, for that will only agitate him. He is glad that the business seems to be improving. Bullets are very bad for business and the shop was not making any money. For many, many long months we lived off the money he had saved. It was a long time and I could see he was a worried man. He is on the roof all the time. Worrying. Walking. And worrying.

He is up on the roof again tonight. He will be restless and will tell me again of the nights of freezing weather when he watched the moon from the trenches, wondering if it would be the last time he would be washed in its light. He told me about the new paint in the store yesterday. I will ask more about that. It will take his mind off the bad things that swish around in his head.

16

Aadil

What? You judge me? You think you would be so different?

I am telling you my story so you can know what choices we have to make each day. Mine were not those of which train to catch or which pizza to buy. The choices I made were the hard ones about whether my family would live or die. They were about whether *I* lived or died.

You think I was irresponsible for taking my son to the station to do that test? You cannot say no, for I see it in your eyes. I would not take him if I really thought he would be killed or harmed. Having the test in that large crowd would make the Americans careful. We were safe. No? How would you have run a test then? No, I thought so.

You judge me, safe on the other side of those bars. If I was a lesser man I would spit in your face. Do not argue with me or you will get no more for your story. My wounds and my death are my condemnation, and you do not yet know how I was wounded. We will learn soon enough how I am going to die. Are you ready? You want me to continue? Good. No more judgment then. You listen. I will talk.

All of the cell-phone triggers had been built and sent off. Fifty is a lot of triggers and I was thinking they would do a good job of keeping the war up to the Americans. I told myself it is one way to fight even though I am no longer in the army. In my heart of hearts, though, I knew this was my only way to make money to look after my family. Every time I sat down to a meal with all those children I was reminded of how much I needed to provide. Such a short time ago I had no worries like this, and nor would I have allowed the children to assist us with their menial jobs.

It would have been good to be a school teacher because that was something I had grown to love. But the school was not able to pay me and I needed to get money from somewhere. And the boys in the classes were benefiting from my money too. They were getting all the experiments in their lessons paid for out of my own pocket and that of Mr Winston. There were many thousands of dollars from Mr Winston for the cell-phone triggers. And each radio trigger was worth more money than I was ever paid in a whole year in the army. So there was a lot I was able to do for the boys at school. That was what I told myself then, and it was how I told myself that this was an acceptable war and that the money was clean money. I was fighting a good cause and the benefits were good for my family and the school.

I had not seen a Winston packet for a long time. Maybe it was three months after I had handed over the cell triggers and two of the radio triggers. Then crumpled Winston appeared on my doorstep full of money. I put the packet in my pocket and later examined it for instructions. There were none but I went that evening to Saleh's café. Halim was there. He was looking clean-shaven and relaxed and he had the shadow of a smile on his face. It was not the sinister smile I had seen before, but the beneficent face I first saw, the face of a prophet. But by now I had better insight into the flinty heart of this man, and his indifference to his fellow believers told me there was a streak hidden there which required me to walk with care. So I did not relax but remained as careful as I had ever been.

After the traditional greetings, he did not rush into security or operational talk. You can imagine that his approach only piled nervousness onto care, and care onto worry.

'You are well?'

'Thank you. Yes, I am well.'

'The teaching goes well? You still enjoy that work?'

I searched his eyes and face for any ill motive but I could not detect any. He seemed to be genuinely interested. I used to work with men who were paid to look genuinely interested but this was not one of those. He was not that clever.

'The teaching is my life calling. I think Allah made me for this.'

'Did He not make you for the same reason He made all of us, to be obedient to His will?' His question was spurious.

'Are you obedient to His will?' It was a dangerous question and I regretted it as soon as I asked it. He startled me with the pause he took to think about his answer and with the answer itself.

'I think I am doing His will, yes, I do. I think there is a need to keep any infidel away from our holy sites.'

'That is a good thing to do.' I nodded. '*Any* infidel?'

'Yes, anyone from anywhere. Even those Iraqis who are not believers.'

I could see he was being serious but it was an answer I didn't want to explore any further. It hinted at too many uncomfortable possibilities. 'That is being obedient to His will. There will be no judgment against you for doing that work.'

'I truly hope not. I work every day to ensure there is no judgment against me. Let's talk about other things. I came here tonight to show you a video. It is not very clear. The person who took it did not expect the blast to be so big. But it shows one of our first attacks on the convoys of the infidels. It used one of the cell-phone triggers you made.'

My stomach lurched and twisted. I had seen many people badly wounded and mutilated over the years. I was not sure I wanted to see something I had created cause that hurt directly. Yet this was war and I have to confess I was curious to see how well my designs performed. It was an appeal to the architect and craftsman in me. May God forgive me, for I am a proud man. You see this as I tell you my story.

Would you look at the video? Ha, you shake your head, but you are not being honest with yourself, and I am sad too because clearly you have learned nothing about me. But let's carry on.

I put my skills above the lives of other men. It was a hard lesson and my instruction was only just beginning. Halim reached into a loose canvas bag with tassels hanging off the bottom. It is a safe bag to carry through the roadblocks and checkpoints around this city, for it is not bulky and guards barely look into them. He pulled out a video camera and opened up a flat screen on its side. He pushed some buttons and set it down on the table as the video began to play.

'I have turned the sound off – there are too many people who might hear it and want to see. This is just for you.'

I nodded, mesmerised, not able to take my eyes off the shaky screen. It seemed to have been filmed from a balcony overlooking a main road. There were some plants in the way, but the screen showed the intersection of one of the roads on the outskirts of a city. I could not tell if it was Baghdad. I watched as three armoured personnel carriers rolled through the intersection followed by some semitrailers. Then there were more of the carriers, followed by more semitrailers. Suddenly there was a cloud of dust and a brief flash of flame and the third semitrailer was struck by a blast strong enough to slam it across the road and into buildings that lined the side. The shock wave struck the person who was filming and the camera dropped to the ground. It filmed the sky and some of the plants for a few seconds before it was picked up and focused again on the burning truck. While other semitrailers kept travelling through the intersection, two armoured personnel carriers stopped to pull the driver from the wreckage. It was hard to tell if he was alive but soon the traffic was gone and all that remained was the burning truck. A few people could be seen peering out from side streets in the last seconds before the video suddenly changed to a blank screen. Halim turned it off, folded the screen and returned the camera to his bag.

'Your devices allow us to attack the Americans. You have done a good thing.'

I was worried. 'I cannot tell you where and how to use these things. But were there not potentially Iraqi casualties in what I have just seen? If there were not casualties, they could still lose their livelihoods?'

Halim nodded. 'That is always possible. But we are careful not to hurt believers. Before that explosion we warned people to leave the area and to stay off the street. You saw there were no people in the area.'

'The Americans will think that is unusual and be on their guard.'

'If they were, then we were still able to attack them.'

I sipped my coffee. There was something else that concerned me.

'What about the convoy? Would it be better to attack the front and middle or the middle and rear, then destroy what is trapped in the middle? One truck alone is hardly a worthwhile target.'

'I see you are thinking like a military man. We plan to do what you say. But this attack was an operational test. We wanted to see how well your devices worked and to show you how effective they are.'

He stood to leave. 'It is excellent work you have done. We like that you are diligent for us. We also like that you work at the school. We know where to find you if we need your help again.' Then he was gone. No smile. Just as it was in the beginning.

I walked to the school next morning and pondered his parting words. They were not the words of a friend. They were the words of a creditor to a debtor. But I had other things to do that day. That day a young man was talking to the boys about peace and reconstruction. About how to get on with your neighbours, especially your big neighbours, the countries that share your borders and who trade and form alliances with you. He was a young man who was coming from the Foreign Ministry. He would be wearing one of his new white shirts with the sapphire-blue cufflinks. He was my nephew and I have great hopes for him. He will do well for Iraq. I hoped the boys might be inspired by Tawfik.

17

Malik

'I miss the moon.'

'The moon?'

'Yes, I miss the moon. Somehow this rooftop is a calmer place under a full moon. The frogs sing and the crickets chorus when there is a moon. There is a hum I can feel across the city when the moon is up.'

'I know what you mean. Tonight it is darker. It is just as hot. It is just as dusty. But somehow the friendliness of the night goes with the moon.'

'But the watcher is here instead.'

'The watcher?'

'When the moon is gone the stars are clearer and one of those is the night star. I do not know which one is the night star, but we can see more stars with the moon down. Perhaps not in summer like now, when the dust and haze reflect the city lights back onto us. But when

the cold winds from the north blow everything clear.
Then the watcher is present.

'By heaven and the night star!
And what shall teach thee what is the night star?
The piercing star!
Over every soul there is a watcher.'

Saleema laughs her soft laugh and leans on my back. 'You
are a strange man. But I am glad of that. You care about
things, like our family. And you think deeply about
things like the watcher. Who remembers obscure verses
like that from the Book?'

'I do. Fragments come to mind when I am sitting up
here wondering if we are all going to survive. But the
Book makes difficulties for me too.'

My wife shifts and I sense she is not comfortable with
what I have said.

'God knows our thoughts. He knows I respect Him.
I just think we are meant to love this present life more
than we do. But we are taught to love the life to come
even more than this one. Does that mean I am not to
make this a better one? What does it mean if I do not
love it? I cannot help myself. I want to love this life. I
want to grasp it tight and make the lives of other people
better because I love this one so much.

If I did not care about this place I could fight and be
killed and go to heaven and then have a better existence.
But that would mean everyone I love here would be

sad. That would not be helping my neighbour. I think of Mahrus. He is a good man and he sweetens my life. I help him and I think I make his life better. We are told to be good to our neighbour, including those who live in other countries. How can we be good to them if we do not love this present life? And how do we improve things if we do not love this present life?'

In the silence that follows the crickets pick up their pulsing chorus and we sit leaning together in the velvet dusty darkness with the flickering orange light of the distant refinery bouncing off the walls.

'You think too much,' she says softly. 'But you think well. These are the things we should be pondering. Imagine if we thought we were only made for the next life. How would a Sunni like you and a Shia like me ever get married? How would any person be able to tolerate another? We would hate and never help our brothers and sisters. We would all be rushing to the next life and not caring what happens in this one.'

'And that could only mean the next one will be worse. For if you arrive in the next one having mistreated other people then you will be severely punished.'

'Unless you have defended the faith by killing unbelievers?'

'No, I do not believe that. God's Book says God will deal with the unbelievers. He does not say we have to kill them. But even if we are instructed to do that, how could such things make this life any better? What if I found a neighbour who was not a believer and I killed him? What if I killed him one day before he planned to become a believer? This would be intolerable and we would all go mad and be deeply suspicious of each other. I prefer another view from the Book – that every day we are the flower of this present life in the lives of the people we meet. I am the flower of this present life for Mahrus. He is my flower. As are you. And the children. And the children of our neighbour, who go to school hand in hand each day even though there are many bombs. The guards who wash puppies. Hard men who soften when they have a chance to preserve a reptile. These are flowers too. That teacher who inspires our boy to study and to love learning. He is a big flower. Soon there is a garden of flowers that make life in this city our new Eden.'

Saleema sighs and murmurs, 'It is a nice picture you paint in your head. Is this what you think when you drive past all those American guns? All those infidels. Are they not poison to those flowers you create in your head? And if you are kind to the Americans, what about their guns? Don't the guns you see every day and which point at you and follow you up the street, don't those guns poison your flowers?'

The shadows of the eucalypts across the road shift slightly and the leaves shuffle against each other. In the daylight they are dusty and grey from sand. In the dark they are light, swishing brushes of percussion as the breeze picks up and moves their skirts about.

'No, these cannot be poison. You see what I am trying to say. If everyone is a flower in the life of someone else then there can be no poison. I have to believe the young soldiers I see out there are not trying to be poison in my life but a flower. That helps me drive past them every day. I still worry about an accident. I think by an accident one of those soldiers might kill me. But I do not think that they will kill me because they hate me.'

'This is too serious. Tell me about Mahrus. He is still lecturing in his shop?'

I laugh and turn around to face Saleema in the dark. I can barely make out the shine in her eyes and the hair whipping about her face in the breeze. Up here in the dark she can have her head uncovered and not worry about what people think. It is private but in the open too.

'Mahrus is now the central attraction in the street. He is the main flower, a bush covered in beautiful buds. He is busier than ever. Many young men come from the Ministry in the middle of the day, but especially at the end of the day, to hear what he has to say. He has vast experience and knowledge. He knows much about people, different cultures and the way foreigners think. The young men are fascinated by him. He starts lots of arguments when he tells them the Americans are men just like them, trying to do their jobs. They threaten never to drink his coffee again. He laughs at them and invites them to issue him with a manly threat, not a threat from a woman. They get excited and even shout when he insults them in this way. Then he calmly tells them he is surprised they are hoping to be diplomats. That stops them in their tracks and they order more coffee. I think

they are getting more instruction from Mahrus than they
are getting in the Ministry. It's a vibrant place and they
still buy shirts. It's coming good.'

'It sounds to me like these young men are his flowers.'

'Aha, so you do think my flower concept works!'

'Don't get too excited. I am just trying to get inside
your head.'

'Well, these men who sit with Mahrus and talk politics
and religion and international affairs, these young men
are truly his flowers. But, you see, they are all flowers, the
men and Mahrus. Each one is bringing light and colour
and pleasure to the other.'

'I'm glad. Maybe I can visit the shop again. It has been
a long time since I've been down there. I would like to
see the new paint and glass.'

I pause. Is that safe? I feel it is safe for myself but this
is the real test. Would I be happy to take my wife and
children to the shop? I am not so sure.

'Let me think about that. Maybe if we get there very
early in the morning, before it gets too hot and too busy.
That would be safe.'

'I am sure it is safe if we stay away from the dangerous
areas.'

'That is the trouble. There are no safe areas and no
dangerous areas. Every incident is random.'

We sit in silence for another twenty minutes until the
hot breeze has stirred up enough sand and dust to drive us
inside. That night I have not seen any falling flares from
the helicopters. I have heard a fast jet speed through the

sky high above us, but there has been nothing happening down here on the ground. The higher the aircraft fly, the safer I feel we are. When helicopters are right over my house I do not feel safe. Unseen and unheard is good for me. We descend the stairs into the heat of the house.

18

Malik

'I had a very interesting day at school just recently, Mahrus. I meant to tell you about it.'

'At school? What were you doing at school?'

'Not any school. The school of my uncle.'

'Your uncle owns a school?'

'No, no, you clown. He teaches there.'

'You have not mentioned family who are teachers. I thought I had heard about your family. They are all Party men and in the military or some part of government we did not want to know about.'

'And the less said about that is still the best policy, Mahrus. I do not want that sort of news being told to everyone. We are changing this country. But this city remains as dry and as flammable as those eucalypts that grow like weeds around this town. It takes so little to incite anyone.'

Mahrus leans in his doorway as Tawfik loosens his

cuffs and removes his tie then sits down. 'I will get some hot coffee and some of those honey chocolates you like. But I would remind you I am not any clown. My shoes fit and my hair is not white. I am a serious man, my young friend.'

'We all are, Mahrus, we all are. But I see the others coming. Maybe they will help us be less serious.'

'Ya, those young men together with the crazy shirt-seller in the shop next door who has been telling me lately we are flowers.' He cackles as he scratches himself, and stretches. 'That shirt-seller, he has some idea he can make each person feel better about each day and be kinder to the other people they meet.'

If Mahrus would ever bustle he does so now, shuffling into the shop to brew more coffee. He, too, has caught sight of the young men coming his way and wants to make the most of their time with him.

Tawfik turns and asks if I will be joining them this afternoon. 'We are all out here, not inside, buying your shirts. You might as well join us.'

'Thank you, I will join you. Just as soon as my wife has finished rearranging things in my shop. She is here to see what I have done with the glass and the paint over the last few months, and now she wants to add her touch.'

Tawfik laughs and slaps his knee. 'You know, they are wanting to help but you cannot admit that. Yet it is good that she thinks it is safe to be out here.'

'She thinks it is safe. I am not so sure, but there have been so few incidents that I can argue against her no more. So down she came with me this morning. Even the American soldier directing traffic at the checkpoint noticed. He was trying to make a joke about me picking up a woman after seeing me drive alone for so long. I told him this was my wife, but he just said it was good I had found a woman and saluted her.'

Tawfik smiles. 'See, even a soldier can be a diplomat.'

By now a small crowd of young men has gathered and are shifting wooden crates and upturned plastic buckets around for seats. They hear me say this about the American soldier and they titter, but some are unsure.

'Was he being disrespectful to your wife?' one asks. 'The Americans can be mistreating of women.' He shakes his head like a sad old wise man.

'No, no, the soldier was respectful. I am thinking he would not have been making jokes six months ago. But today it is more relaxed and the bombings are not so frequent. Even the soldiers such as him are less on edge.'

'Six months is a long time. Is it the same soldier?'

'It is, though he was replaced for a short while. I do not understand how he has been there so long. It is very unusual, but maybe this too is a sign things are improving. The Americans swap their men around so quickly none of them get to know us or the neighbourhood very well. The soldiers are trying to be policemen, but how can they be policemen if they cannot tell the good people from the bad people? This soldier, he knows everyone that passes and he knows the locals too. I think by now he is probably like us and can sense when there is trouble coming. And perhaps he is glad he is not fighting in the south.'

'You have a very odd idea of what a policeman does, Mr Malik. No police I ever met knew who was who in this city. Or rather, I should say they only knew the bad people, the criminals, mainly because they were in business with them.' The young man offering this observation pauses to take his coffee from Mahrus, who has appeared with a tray of cups and dates, which he sets down on the table. There is an uncomfortable silence and some of the young heads shift nervously to look up the street to see if anyone has overheard this seditious remark.

Mahrus wipes his hands on his old towel and regards this future representative of our country.

'Ah, you are still living in the old Baghdad, I see. You cannot yet be diplomats when you look over your shoulder to see if there is anyone offended by what you say.'

'I will not be a diplomat in Baghdad, old man. But you are right, we still reflex for the wrong reasons. Though, you have to admit we do not have a good experience of the police in this town.'

'I have clearly taught you poorly. You should know I'll admit nothing. It's true, however, that the police in other countries are employed to protect the communities they live in. Our police are employed to protect the government. The question for you is, what is the government being protected from in such a case as ours? Or in Iran? Or Kuwait? Or any of our neighbouring states?

Why are our police different from the ones in America or Europe? Who are the enemies of our police?'

I think we all know the answer to that, so the response from one of the young men surprises me.

'From foreign enemies who hate us. That is who they protect us from.'

Mahrus lifts an eyebrow and the boy knows he is in trouble. 'Our police protect us from these people. So that is why our country is flooded with foreigners walking around with weapons and Iraqis are not?' Mahrus shakes his head. 'No, not even in Iraq were the police responsible for checking foreign enemies. That is for the army and other unseen forces none of us really know about but which we have grown to fear. Our police, as we knew them before the Americans came, and as I fear they will remain, are designed to protect the government from its own people. Go and be diplomats in your new postings and study your host country and the role their police play. It will tell you a lot about the leadership of the country. What their police do will tell you if their leaders are able to sleep innocent sleep or not. And if not you should worry about why not.'

The young men sit looking at Mahrus as if they have heard a new thing for the first time. As indeed they probably have. They have grown up knowing only one sort of law enforcement. An invisible but feared police is normal for them. Some shake their heads in surprise.

Mahrus picks up the tray of dates and offers it around. 'Here you are, please …'

The rolling boom carries across the city and cuts him short. Instinctively we all look up in the direction of the sound, which echoes downriver, slides into every lane, presses each pane of glass, and sinks into the heart of every person within earshot. Not once but three times. Heavy, resonating echoes like the drumming beats of doors slammed shut with a solid bang. We turn towards the source as if in obedient worship to a malevolent god who demands attention each time he claps his hands.

'… eat all these dates. They have been in my shop for far too long.'

'I always knew you were trying to poison us, Mahrus. Why do you think we stayed away for so long? It was not the bombs or the shooting.'

'For you, coffee will be last,' pronounces Mahrus, as he starts to pour the yellow liquid into the small tumblers and hand them around. 'Let us drink and listen to what Tawfik was going to tell us about his day at school. Let us hear something positive and not think about bombs or death or our policemen. Please, Tawfik, tell us something fresh and enlightening.'

We all look to Tawfik, who is now standing and gazing towards the sound of the blasts. From in front of our shops it is hard to see over the rooftops, and Baghdad is such a flat city. Some of the government buildings give the best view of what is happening across this town. And maybe the bridges, if you are allowed to stop and look. There is no breeze, so there will be a column of smoke and dust marking the site of the explosion, but it is not visible from the street.

'You look worried. That was a long way from here, Tawfik.'

'It was,' he agrees. 'But I can never get used to these things. Every time there is an explosion I think of the ruination of the lives of ordinary people. I think that the work I do for Iraq is meaningless overseas if there is killing and destruction here. How can I build Iraq when others are tearing it down?'

Mahrus hands him a hot tumbler and presses the tray of dates on him. And some advice. 'When there are more builders than destroyers then the builders eventually overcome.'

'Only as long as the builders are more patient than the destroyers. Those who destroy too often have more zeal than the builders. The builders eventually leave when they see their efforts torn down.'

'And that is you?'

'No, that is not me. Never!' The gleam in Tawfik's eyes tells us that he is resolved to not give up. I hope for all of us that people like Tawfik will not give up.

'So come now, tell us about school.'

Tawfik is glad to change the subject. I can see that. He helps himself to a date, holding it up to us between thumb and forefinger, and poses a question to us all.

'This humble seed is in the kitchens of the Middle East, the Americas and Europe. It is cooked in every place in the world. Yet who in all those places knows that we in Iraq produce and export more of these than anyone else? Iraq is in the kitchens of the whole world. How do we tell others that we are not bad people and that we too desire peace?'

'Used to be the largest exporter,' growls Mahrus. 'Until all this madness started.'

'Not so, not so,' replies Tawfik as he places the date in his mouth and starts chewing. 'Production and exports have declined but we are still the world's largest exporter of dates. That tells you how many of these we used to export. Now we need to export our message to the world. And that is my new job.'

'Tell us about the school, Tawfik, we know all about your new job and the crusade you are on.'

The boys guffaw at the good-natured gibe and Tawfik smiles.

'I was asked by my uncle to speak to a class of boys. My uncle used to be in the military but lost his job in 2003 when the new administration took over and sacked anyone in the Ba'ath Party. He has struggled since then, but he must have had some savings because he still keeps his family fed. Recently he started teaching. He is an engineer, you see. He knows all sorts of things and can teach chemistry and physics. Since he has been teaching, he has had more money to feed his family and that has been good for him. But I think the teaching has given him a purpose as well.'

'Is he a crusader like you, Tawfik? Maybe he can join us at the Ministry?' They all laugh.

'No, he was a military man, as I said. The military is not usually a good place for moral crusaders.'

'A military man now teaching? That is not such a crazy thing.'

'You are right. That is a very acceptable thing. But it was interesting for me to hear what the boys in his class were thinking. We have a generation of children that are trying to understand what it means to be an Iraqi. They do not understand how to be a citizen in their own country.'

'What do you mean?' I am intrigued and alarmed all at once. The children in this city, including my own, are my flowers. I hope they are not about to be poisoned by what young Tawfik has to say.

'They come to school with their satchels, and some even have books. They talk about what they have seen on television and read in books and heard from their families. What they see on television can be bad. Some of them watch television channels out of Europe, which are full of sex. That is immoral. Others watch television channels from around the Middle East and see and hear all the killing. That is bad too. Some watch children's programs from around the world. From America. From Canada. From England. That is not evil, but it is not good either.'

'Why do you say the children's programs are bad?' I ask. 'I understand that if they are watching news from around the region it can be bad. Or that they are seeing evil things on television that Allah would hate, then that is bad. But children's programs? That cannot be harmful.'

'Maybe not harmful but it means they are talking and thinking like foreigners in their own country. Not like Iraqis. I thought it was interesting these young people have a strong view about foreigners. How many children in any country would know who their neighbours are? Who their enemies are? How many know about other countries around the world? I am surprised to find our own Iraqi children know more about the countries around us, especially the ones that have attacked us, than about Iraq. None of the boys I talked to knew anything about our ancient history, that we live on the location of old cities built before time, or that Adam was made and lived in this part of the world. But they were eager to know these things. So I told them about the place Iraq will have in the world. A place in the sun. A place of peace. A place where people can come to understand their ancient roots, for we all come from this Eden between the Euphrates and the Tigris. From this dust Adam was made and all of us from here too.'

Tawfik helps himself to another date. 'One day we will be known not for our enormous date production but as the centre of civilisation, and our people will be civilised people again.'

'Your uncle – he is Mr Aadil?'

'Yes, his name is Aadil.' He is a little guarded. 'You know him?'

'I do not know him well, but he teaches my boy. I was in the classroom recently when the boys showed us what he had taught them. Chemistry and biology and physics and lots of other things. I think the boys love that he was once in the army. He tells stories about tanks and planes and things which fascinate young boys but which are not yet understood by them. I think he is a good teacher and told him so. My son is excited to go to school and to be taught by him.'

Tawfik folds his hands behind his head. 'Thank you, that is nice to hear. It is good he is doing well after the army. He teaches those boys as best he can about everything except how to fight. And he is teaching them how to be at peace with their neighbour. He is teaching them how not to hate.'

Saleema has been standing shyly in the doorway of our shop, listening to the conversation. She speaks now and surprises us all.

'That is the hardest thing. Teaching them not to hate when they see so much hate around this city. What is that bomb earlier if it is not hate?' None of us has any sensible answer and the conversation around the coffee and dates falls silent.

19

Aadil

I was hoping I would not see a Winston packet again. Alarmingly there had been the usual bombs exploding around the city but few were directed at the Americans. There are many groups in this city trying to attack the Americans and to drive them out, but not many attacks are coordinated. It was hard enough to do this when we were a single army with communications connecting us all. Now there are no communications other than those that are spoken. Few communications are written.

I should have been paying more attention to my descent, for I had delivered the cell-phone triggers and now six of the radio triggers had gone. I did not need to design anything else. But I had been bought and knew there was no way I could escape these men. I could not return the money. The best I could hope for was that they would not ask me to work for them again. When the

Winston packet reappeared on the front doorstep I was dismayed. Halim asked to meet at the usual place.

He gave me good reason to be concerned. He behaved like a dog with fleas, jumping without warning to look into every dark corner in case something or someone posed a threat. He made me nervous by drawing attention to us like this. Tonight he was a lieutenant of someone he feared – a small man with one leg. Well, he had two legs but one was made of aluminium. A bald and clean-shaven man – square-shouldered and who walked without the usual limp or throw of the hip typical of an amputee. He walked like a man possessed of a jinn, propelling himself forward with energy and speed. None should get in his way.

There was no introduction when the man arrived, just a tilt of the chin in my general direction, then Halim left and sat on the path outside, while the short man in the shiny brown suit seated himself at the table, half facing me and half watching the doorway.

'You are Colonel Aadil?'

'I am Aadil,' I corrected.

'You have resigned your commission?'

'No.'

'Then you are Colonel Aadil, are you not?'

'I am only a colonel when the government recognises I am a colonel. Until then I am Aadil and I teach at the junior high school.' This was not going well.

He peered at me for a long time then retrieved his briefcase from under the table where he had placed it moments before. Opening it he withdrew a small camera and slid it across the table. I could guess what was going to happen next.

'We are happy with the work you have done. What we have paid you has been money well spent. The Americans thwart many of the explosions in this city. So we are forced to use martyrs to help our cause against them. That was until your triggers came along. We will use them quickly, for soon there will be countermeasures against them. Then we will need your help again.'

'You will need my help for as long as the Americans are here. What happens after they have left and we are settled in our own land? You will have no need of me then.'

'Maybe you will be back in your army. Safe again.'

I did not like his tone but I had no particular argument with him just then. Besides his hand was poised over the video and the sooner I saw what he wanted me to see then the sooner I would be rid of him.

'We are learning to attack the Americans where they are most vulnerable and weak, and they are most vulnerable and weak where they are trying to protect their friends. Their Iraqi friends are our enemies. So we are attacking anyone who helps them. The Americans hate being made to choose and when they do they often choose poorly. In turn that undermines Iraqi confidence in their American friends. Soon the Iraqi parliament will be forced to ask the Americans to leave. Then we can secure Iraq for Iraqis.' I knew I was not going to like what I was about to see.

The video was taken from a vehicle at some distance away from the target – a suburban police station. It was one of the recently refurbished buildings the Americans had started to reoccupy. A collection of people milled about. Small cars drove in and around it after being checked by guards. Concrete barriers prevented larger vehicles from getting too close. Two American armoured personnel carriers, with their long cannons probing into the street, stood guard. There was no flash. One second just a typical street scene and in the next instant a boiling cloud of dust out of which bounced pieces of brick and mortar. Unlike Halim, this man left the sound turned on. Over the crack of the bomb could be heard the video recordist repeating *Allahu Akbar*, as though perhaps seeking atonement for what he had just witnessed.

The short man paused the video. 'You see what exploded?'

I shook my head. 'It was not possible to tell. But I do not think it was any of the cars.'

'Very good, very good. No, it was one of the concrete barriers that was placed there a month ago. Placed there with one of your triggers and left dormant for that period of time. We hoped no one would crash into it. No one did. The concrete barrier was not fully concrete but cast with just an outer shell and the explosive in the middle. Clever, no?'

I nodded. It was clever, but this sort of warfare was too full of people being exceptionally clever, and it was the clever ones who stayed safe. Those who ran messages, carried out the bidding of unseen commanders, built electronics and bombs, well, only those are the ones who die. I pushed that thought to the back of my mind and left it alone, but I see you agree. I pushed it to one side and asked about other things that concerned me. 'Did the personnel carriers survive? What happened to them? A concrete barrier can be indiscriminate. There were many police around their new station and people coming to them for help.'

He said nothing as he resumed playing the video. Out of the cloud of dust I could see the carriers move forward and take up positions to block the street. Their occupants would be badly shaken but they were intact. As I watched, the cloud of dust disappeared and I could see burning vehicles, and soon the collapsed front of the police station, though no fire yet. Four or five bodies lay face down in the debris. I knew from experience there would be a similar number of unseen bodies broken up across the ground. Thankfully the resolution of the camera did not allow me to see that. He switched the camera off and placed it in the briefcase.

'This is the second video you have shown me. I have seen this one for what reason?'

'I want you to know that we appreciate your work. That it is valuable and that we will call on you to do more. But also to let you know we keep good records. All the phone numbers. All the part numbers you are supplied. And videos of each time your triggers are used. We take no risks, you know.'

I was surprised for a moment before I remembered these people were nurtured in a culture of fear and mistrust. Iron rods and blood were used to bind allegiances between these men, and he was only behaving as he had been trained. But that calm understanding in my head did not quell the fury in my stomach. I was very angry with him, though I did not shout or bang the table in the way one of my sergeants may once have done.

'You enlist my help, which I willingly give, then you threaten me in order to keep that help. You have a poor understanding of how to lead people. Manipulation and threats will only take you so far.'

He held my gaze and did not seem perturbed. He was the one with the power. He knew I depended on him and could never really defy him. He understood my weakness. 'We know you are working at the school. And that you are preferring that work to what you did for us. In case you go soft on us we need to ensure your loyalty.'

He pushed himself to his feet and paused to steady himself. 'I trust that is the case.'

I was careful. 'That will depend on the terms. I will not be manipulated but I am always prepared to negotiate.'

He lifted an eyebrow at me then stalked out, joined by Halim as he departed. I rubbed my chin. The short man had revealed something he had perhaps not intended. All of the suppliers of electronic components were wittingly complicit in the web of weapons construction. They had to be if they were able to log component numbers and keep track of my purchases.

Then I was startled by something else. I have told you Saleh is a quiet man. We had not spoken, other than in a cursory way, during visits to his café for meetings with Halim, though like any businessman in this town he was vigilant and tracked who walked in and out of his shop. I knew he always watched me. That was what he was trained to do. Watch people. Observe and note. Think about what he has seen and heard. Always vigilant under his humble thatch and lowly station. He watched but did not ever speak about what he saw. Until now, and what he had to say changed everything.

'Mr Aadil, we know each other reasonably well. We are nearly neighbours. I admire what you are doing at the school. A demonstration involving the boys like that was very unusual.'

'But effective?'

'Yes, very effective. I watched those boys that morning. You have earned their respect, not out of fear, but out of love for you.'

What could I say? So I said nothing and Saleh pushed on.

'I admire your work and we are as good as neighbours. Yet I need to share some things with you, things you may not like. I would be no true neighbour if I let you walk these streets ignorant of the things I have heard.'

I must have reacted, perhaps in an aggressive way. He stepped back one pace and put up a hand. 'Don't be afraid. I'm not your enemy. We know each other from those years when we worked for our government. You have seen me with the other parents in your classroom. My children have been killed in this war but my nephews are in your class. My brother is dead also. I came to be their father. I know you do good things for the boys. And I know you are a decent man. You wanted to be a good leader when you were an officer and I know you want to be a good father to your family. I see you try to be a good man for your neighbours. I see that generator as an example of your heart.' He dropped his hand and moved closer to wipe the table.

'So all these months I see you come and go with Halim and I think, "Something is not right." But I keep my mouth shut. Yes, I know him. I see him talk and you listen. That is strange to me and I suspect you are contracted to him. But I know Halim. He is a criminal. Petty. But still a criminal. I ask myself why is Aadil answering to a man who was never in the military. When he should have been serving his country he was in Dubai and Kuwait. Smuggling and doing things that are bad for our country and for our people. When I saw you with him it made no sense. But it was not major crime and, besides, in this town these days you keep your mouth shut, no?'

'You keep your mouth shut. That is wise advice.'

'Tonight I am going to open my mouth because I think you are a good man. For your class. For our neighbourhood. For our boys. And because I want to believe you are not a criminal. I want to know my assessment of you all those years ago holds good. Do you know the man whom Halim brought to you tonight?'

'No, I have never met him before.'

'And yet you associate with him? Are seen with him?' Saleh could not hide his indignation.

'Well, I hardly had a choice. And no, as I have already said, I had not met him before.'

'And you did not check beforehand who he is?'

'Come now, how could I do that? But you sound as if you know him. What are you concerned about?'

Saleh shook his head at me and I heard the disdain in his reply. 'This man is no good. I know him from another time. He has forgotten. I was not important to him then. There are in fact many who know him. He cannot see those of us he thinks have sunk below him. He thinks he can swim through here without anyone recognising him, but he is wrong.'

'This man has a name?'

'Nothing that will help. Mohammed. But I know where he lives.'

I filed that information away and left it alone for the moment. 'Why are you so agitated about him?'

'I hear things. Whispers on the street. My sources are good, you should expect that.'

I nodded. 'You hear whispers? Does that mean you have no proof?'

'I don't always need proof. Some details just add up and a picture forms. Call it intuition. But what I hear fits this type of man.'

'And that is?'

'Come now!' Saleh could barely hide his derision. 'He is a confidant of Halim, that is enough to start with, is it not? Pigs consort with pigs, never with antelope.'

I resisted. I had to. Saleh was in earnest but I didn't want to hear anything that undermined what I had been doing.

'No one should be condemned by the company he keeps. Besides, I understand he has been doing good work against the Americans. That is a noble cause, surely?' Yet, it was an argument that sounded hollow even as I marshalled it.

Saleh merely snorted.

'He tells people he is attacking Americans and is fighting for Iraq. He has never attacked anything except a target that will deliver him money or revenge. If he tells you he is attacking Americans, you can know he is lying. The lie is believed by so many people.'

'The lie?'

'Yes, the lie.' Saleh could not help himself and he leaned forward and glared at me. 'The lie that all these bombings are directed at the Americans. The lie that we are at war with America. Then the other lies, that we fight among ourselves, Sunni against Shia, everyone against the Kurds. That is all lies for the foreign press, but they tell us those lies too.

'What idiots do they think I am? You think I don't recognise a lie when I see it? They take me for a fool. And they play you for one too, if you believe everything you are told.'

'Saleh, you are talking in a way that troubles me. You are saying the man I am meeting with is not working against the Americans?'

He made no effort to hide his scorn. In another life I could have had him arrested for his derogatory tone.

'You were a senior man in the army. You are not a stupid man. But today I hear you say stupid things. I am telling you as a favour, and because I think you are a decent man, that the person you are dealing with is nothing more than a petty criminal turned to big crime, and who has never fought an American in his life. He is a coward dog who runs from anyone who stands up to him. And the Americans are too hard a target for him. He would never directly take them on in a fight because they fight back. Hard and fierce. That man who pays you will never grab the hornet that will sting him.'

He stepped to a nearby table and wiped it down.

I hissed at his back, 'You know this for sure?'

He finished wiping the table and turned back. His tone was softer.

'No, no. To be honest I don't know this for sure. I told you I hear whispers. I would lie to you if I told you I had hard proof. I don't have a forensic file of evidence. But I have my instincts and I know they are true. I will keep listening and I will keep talking to you about this man, if I hear or see anything else. But you should test your heart. See if what I say is true. Don't take this person at face value, because men like him place no value in you other than how you assist with the crimes they pursue. As for fighting Americans – pfft, they are less than women and worse than dogs. They would never dare such a thing.'

With that he went back to the bar and I left for my home. I was alert to being watched, but if Mohammed had any of his people around me I did not see them. There was little need for them to follow me. If they could place Mr Winston on my doorstep whenever they pleased, then there was no point in tailing me all over the city. Nonetheless, I was nervous and vigilant. And as I picked my way from shadow to shadow through the lanes and alleyways in that warm, dusky night I was filled with rage.

As much as I did not want to admit it, Saleh was right. These men had none of the qualities I would expect from true warriors. The painful truth was not that I had been lied to. What hurt was that I had allowed myself to believe the lie. I, not Halim, was the ignoble one. I had been manipulated and I was angry at believing the lie, for I had known in my heart of hearts this was where it would end up. I was furious I had been disrespected when I was dismissed without cause from the army. I was angry that I had been forced to beg for this job so I could feed my family. I was angry that I had allowed myself to believe the fabric of a story that was so full of holes there was no safety in it. I had been treated with dishonour. In the end I was betrayed.

20

Malik

If a bomb is big and nearby I see the windows in my room flex inwards. I know from what I have seen in the street that many people die from the wounds of glass, metal and stones. They bleed to death in seconds after being cut up by these small things. In my house we have small windows but they still have a lot of glass that can hurt us. So we leave the windows open just a little, even in winter. If a blast is nearby, the windows will swing inwards and the glass will not break. We also have the curtains made of heavy material. It is strange to have them hanging in the windows in the middle of summer but we keep them drawn and hope they will slow some of the shards. Many friends have put shutters over their windows. We have a middle room in our house where there are no windows. Just to be safe.

This morning there is a blast which is close. I can feel it before I hear it. The curtains shift in the room as if on a breeze, though the day is still and hot. I run up the stairs to the roof immediately. A small black column of dust and smoke climbs into the sky from a few suburbs away. Already the military helicopters are swinging past the area but not getting too close. Once a bomb has exploded there are two possible consequences. A second bomb explodes, designed to attack any military and police forces arriving to work on the scene. Or there is nothing and the single bomb was all there was meant to be. In each scenario it is not helpful to have the helicopters get too close. They can be shot at, or else there is nothing for them to do. But they circle anyway. Maybe they are filming. Or maybe they are hoping to see the attackers.

After taking my eyes off the helicopters, I scan across the rooftops, through the aerials and the palm trees, trying to make out exactly where the blast has taken place. It is hard to see but I slowly realise it is near the local mosque. My heart starts to beat more quickly and my stomach turns over a few times in worry. If the explosion was directed at the military, then Iraqis are likely to be safe. If the attack was one religious group against another, then anyone could be hurt. I am disappointed too. An attack on a mosque means the streets will be full of people shouting at each other. It will not be safe for my boy to go to school. Not today. Not for a week, maybe, since he has to walk past that mosque to get to his class.

Just as I am starting to think that this city was getting better. There have not been so many explosions, business is better and Mahrus is feeling safer in the street. I do not want us to go backwards. I want us to go forwards. The young men who talk to Mahrus are right: we are the most ancient of ancient civilisations. We can be the model of civilisation to the whole world. But not if we treat each other like savages.

I go downstairs and tell Saleema the children should be kept at home today. She understands. I ask the neighbour's guard, wandering the street, to make sure Imaad and his sisters stay in the compound. They are not to leave, not even for the puppies. They can play with them when I come home. He agrees. I drive the Datsun extra carefully this morning. The city is on edge. The American at the checkpoint has his rifle up again. Today he does not smile.

As I open the shop, Mahrus enters with a silver tray bearing coffee and dates spread out for me. He speaks kindly and I am glad of his encouragement on this day. He is such a special friend, a flower, a bright one with petals that never fade.

'You will be having a sorry day today, Malik, my friend.'

'You know me better than a brother.'

'We are brothers of the street, born of the street and all it has taught us. And this street, in particular, has taught us that there can be pain on the days when we think there should be no pain.'

I sip the coffee. It is spicy and hot and refreshing and I am glad of that. The leathered lines around Mahrus's eyes pull his face into a pleasant and open expression. That is the great blessing of this man.

'No windows missing in the shop today. That is a good thing.'

I have to agree. 'Yes, anything that does not kill us or remove our livelihood is good for us. But I wonder if the audience that sits at your feet each day will not gather this morning. I think that blast was at the mosque. I cannot be sure, but if it was, then they may not come. It only takes one incident to disrupt our lives precariously.'

Mahrus nods. 'Yes, the whisper that has passed up and down the street this morning is that the mosque was attacked. Many men are wounded who were coming to the second prayer. It exploded just as they were gathering around the doors. You know how we do – stopping to talk and tell stories before going inside to pray. Very sad. The pious who pray to Allah and pray His blessing on us all are the ones who are dead this morning.'

'I do not understand how that helps us. That sort of action will not make the Americans leave any faster than they might have been planning. An explosion in front of the mosque helps the Americans stay. It gives the Americans cause to say to the Iraqi government that they need as much help as they can get.'

Mahrus pours me more coffee. 'It is a crazy bombing that helps nobody and only increases the misery for us all. We Iraqis must stop this madness. Until we do the Americans will stay.'

21

Aadil

The number of boys in the classroom that morning was small. How was it so many were absent? I waited for thirty minutes. I had heard no bombs in my suburb and I had not heard of any bombs going off in other parts of the city. Because Baghdad is flat, on a still morning a big blast can be heard across the whole town. But sometimes, for no sensible reason I can understand, the sound does not carry very far at all. Maybe it is a breeze that pulls the sound away from us. Or maybe we are just too used to hearing them that we fail to notice the rolling booms anymore. But no matter how much I searched my memory I was not able to recall anything that morning that sounded or felt like a bomb. Sometimes it's just a feeling, you know.

You look at me blankly. I do wonder how you got a journalist's pass. But the feeling is a real thing. I know you Westerners do not believe in feelings or dreams or even God. But these are real things and tell us a story. And I am engineer enough to know a blast far away can signal a message across a vast distance and be channelled down long streets. A tremor in your skin, a ripple in the air, a faint fracture across your heart. Something felt yet intangible, but no matter how faint, you know it signals the death of one of our citizens. That morning I had neither heard nor felt anything. Eventually I asked the boys why so many were absent.

'A mosque was bombed this morning. My friends were not allowed to come to school because they had to walk near the mosque,' said one.

'A mosque?'

'Yes, sir, it was a mosque that was attacked. Everyone is angry it was a mosque.'

'Is this true? Has anyone else heard of the bomb?'

'Yes, sir. There are others who cannot come this morning because of the attack. My parents were not wanting to send me to school, but because I could get here with my cousin in his truck I was allowed to come.'

'Was the imam hurt?'

The boys looked at each other and shrugged. 'We do not know, sir. We just know there were some coming to prayer who were killed and some who were injured. My father was upset because the ambulances could not get there quickly and because the Americans did not want to come down the narrow lanes with their tanks to clear the way for the ambulances.'

'We cannot blame the Americans. They might think it is a trap. The first bomb to be followed by other bombs once they are lured down a lane. If I was an American I would stay out of the lanes too.'

'But, sir, they should have helped.'

'Yes, maybe they should have helped. It is hard to say what should have been done because we were not there. It is too easy to make a judgment based on television reports. Unless we are there at the place of the incident there can be no assumption about what we might have done ourselves or what others should have done. That is a lesson in life, not one from the books,' I added in as light a tone as I could muster. 'Let's finish that chemistry experiment with cloth dyeing, shall we?'

The rest of the day went slowly. Rising up into my mind was the dark thought that this attack on the mosque was something of my doing. What if the bomb had been triggered by one of my own designs? What if my triggers were not being used against the Americans, but by Iraqi against Iraqi? What if Saleh was right and I was only helping criminals? Then the awful thought seeped into my mind that some of the fathers of boys in this class could have been injured or killed by my hand. There was no honour in any scenario I could conceive and my mind turned to the shame I might have brought on my family. As the day wore on, my worry became greater. I think the small class was glad to be finished in the end and to be going home.

I waited some time before I went to the coffee shop rather than home. I wanted to know more about Halim and especially the short man he worked for.

Saleh greeted me as I entered and suggested I sit at his counter where he could talk to me directly, still keeping his eye on other customers. It was unusual to be sitting there. But I wanted the conversation to be safe for him.

'You told me you hear a lot about this Mohammed. What do you know? What do you think I should expect from him?'

'I told you what I know. And they are only whispers. I thought you didn't want to know about my whispers.'

I was not of a mind to speak too frankly with Saleh. But I needed to understand what the street was hearing. Call it the last gasp of a betrayed man. Call it anything you like, but I needed to hear from Saleh, a man who dealt in information gleaned from others, just what was carried on the hot zephyrs that swirled the dust up our lanes.

'I need to hear the whispers. I need to hear the stories. I need to understand as best I can what I have been handling before I am tainted beyond redemption.'

'Redemption?' Saleh sounded surprised. 'There is redemption in this place? You are serious, I see. Well, I said to you I wanted to help, so I need to tell you what I hear. Maybe we can both be redeemed in the process.'

'I worry that I am beyond saving. But I won't know until I hear everything I can.'

Saleh served up coffee, wiped his hands and leaned on his counter, watching the doorway and talking softly. 'Mohammed is a man who takes his money from all sorts of people.' He paused. 'Some say he deals with scum in Iran who trade weapons and lives. Others say he smuggles drugs from Dubai, across the water and up to Basra. Ha.' He moved away to serve a customer and picked up minutes later where he had left off.

'All the rumours suggest he makes money out of our miserable turmoil now. A man who creates disturbances so that he can kill his competitors, take revenge on his enemies. Or it can be simply to make a point to the police or security forces or someone in government he wants payment from in order to stop the bombs.'

'You said earlier he did not attack Americans. You said that if he told me he was attacking Americans that I should think he is telling a lie.'

'I think if you and I could test this man' – Saleh lifted a knowing eyebrow at me – 'we would discover this person is a thief and a coward. He is not a man to attack a soldier. He fears the soldier. If the Americans are attacked by someone else then perhaps he will take advantage of that. But he is careful not to directly attack Americans. I hear he sides sometimes with the Shia militia when it is helpful to do so. Outside Baghdad I know he has Sunni allies. He uses anyone he can.'

'What if I told you that I had seen a video showing his forces attacking an American convoy?' I desperately countered.

He was taken aback but only for a moment. 'Did you see that this was a video of his forces attacking the convoy, or did you just see an attack on a convoy?'

I had to think. 'I saw an attack but I did see it on his video camera.' I paused again. 'Though it was an assumption I made that it was his video.'

'You think that if he wanted to attack a convoy he would do it himself? If I gambled, I would bet that he paid someone to do that work for him. He would buy everyone.' He pushed another glass tumbler of hot coffee across the counter to me. 'Has he bought you?'

That struck me hard. If this person was as unscrupulous as Saleh was suggesting then my situation – and that of my family – was more dangerous than I thought.

'I did some work for him. Made him some electronics. Nothing more, nothing less.'

'Does he know where you live?'

'Yes.'

'Does he know where you work?'

'Yes.'

'Does he know where you constructed these electronic pieces?'

I nodded.

'Then you can assume he has bought you. You are a former Ba'ath Party man. You know how these webs work. They either work for you. Or they work against you. But no web can ever be neutral. That is what defines a web, does it not? The hunter or the prey. Nothing in between.'

'You were not always in the coffee business?' I tried not to sound too sarcastic, given we both knew I had an insight into his background.

'None of us are what we seem, as we eke out a living in this place or, as with you, try and make it a better place.'

'I know, I know. But why tell me all this?'

He straightened and glared around his shop, and for a second I saw something of the hard iron in him that must have ensured his safety working inside the machinery of Saddam's regime.

'We have become animals, squabbling in our own filthy sty as the rest of the world looks over the fence and wonders at the behaviour they see. Not just any animals but filthy swine taking money and advice from infidels all over the world. We sell ourselves to the cheapest bidder and that always seems to be another Iraqi. We receive each day from God Himself the judgment we deserve. We can be better than this but only if we stand up to people like Mohammed. And if we take some risks in doing so. For all I know you are his second in command and his most trusted adviser. I do not think so but that is a risk I have taken to stop this man, and stop us slaughtering ourselves. How can we be proud when we are a laughing stock to the world? Sometimes I am ashamed to be called an Iraqi.'

'You think we are filthy? How is that, when all we are doing is defending ourselves?'

He leaned close, his eyes aflame with anger.

'You are no fool. Yet you are a fool if you cannot answer me this! How is it that a six-year-old boy can be killed in this city? How is it that some idiotic militia who has no ideology other than to put their filthy swine snouts in the trough can cook him alive in an oven with onions and tomatoes? How is it that the cooked carcass is left on a steel tray on the front doorstep of his father's house for his family to find? How is it that a note with two words only is pinned to the meat? "Bon appétit?" You can answer me these questions?' he hissed, his rage barely contained and his nose close to mine. I had no answer, though I knew this story well. Who in their heart of hearts could explain such a thing?

'No, I thought not. We are become Satan ourselves. Satan does not wait for us in Gehenna. He walks these streets looking like an Iraqi man carrying a gun. We are no civilisation. We are filthy swine and deserve the judgment we are getting. And you are working for one of them. What do you think you are, teaching and killing with the same mouth and same hands? An angel or a devil?'

He did not wait for an answer. The flare went out of his eyes, replaced by tears, and he wiped his brow before walking away to the pavement to take some orders.

'We have become our own judgment,' I muttered to myself as I got up to leave. It struck me deeply. I was shaken and knew I needed to consider what I should do next. As I turned to leave, Saleh bumped into me and muttered final words which struck guilt even deeper. 'The mosque that was bombed. The rumours skittering up the street to me today suggest your new friends were behind that. Revenge against a cleric who denied use of the mosque to hide drugs. This is the calibre of man who pays you. I hear they are boasting about a sophisticated trigger that needed three calls to set it off. You're the engineer. What do you make of that?'

22

Saleema

I live with my husband, Malik, in a neighbourhood where many of my school friends still live. So many of them grew up and married and stayed in the area. But since 2003 some of these girls have moved with their husbands or families away from Baghdad. Some lucky ones are in Jordan or Kuwait. But most still live here. When Malik is at work they come around to our house and we talk about our children and our men. We also talk about clothes. When Saddam was our president we had lots of clothes we could choose from. And we were lucky to be able to get gorgeous silks and cottons and coloured materials from all over the world. Now we talk about the things we would like to have but do not have the chance to own. Some of the girls have asked Malik to buy them special clothes from India when he is buying his shirts but he is embarrassed.

Malik is shy about these things.

'I cannot buy special clothes for other women.'

'Why not? My girlfriends are as good as family.'

'No, on this matter they are not family. It wouldn't be proper for me, trying to hear the will of God and at the same time buying such intimate things. Those are only for a husband to see, not a friend.'

I tell him he is too old-fashioned and surely God would look kindly on any gifts that brought light to his friends, especially his wife. But he is stubborn on this and will not budge. It is too bad for my friends, but they do not miss out completely. I don't tell Malik but I share some of my gifts with them. Silly, kind man. He does not even notice I don't wear them.

Today my dear niece Fatimah is at my house. She walked over early and arrived just as we were waking. The puppies were yapping and squeaking in excitement and we lay awake wondering what had alerted them so. The murmuring tones of the guard assured us all was okay and soon we heard him laughing, followed by the gentle cooing laughter of Fatimah. The guard would have been helpless and hopeless in front of her. He would have been looking at the ground, unsure what to say, and would have done whatever she asked. So much for being the strong man of the neighbourhood. Fatimah with her red hair peeking out from under her chador and her green eyes carefully and expertly decorated with the charcoal and metal makeup colours she loves so much. He would have been no match for her at all if he was trying to prevent her entry to our compound.

Today we spend the day at the house while the children play and Malik is at the store. We talk about nothing and everything, while I braid her hair and we model jewellery on each other and talk some more. Often we talk about how Malik thinks Iraq is becoming a better place at last. We women live in fear for the lives of our children. That can make us think the worst is always about to happen. Fatimah cannot understand the optimism in Malik.

'What does he say about the bombing of the mosque? That cannot be a sign that Iraq is becoming a better place, surely?'

I have to agree but I defend Malik. 'He is saddened by that too. He is worried about the children, so they stay at home. But he will have Imaad back at school as soon as possible. He thinks we are in a better place because his shop is now earning money and because business is thriving on his street. He told me another store near him has reopened this week. These are signs people are becoming more confident, feeling more secure and safe.'

'Unless they worship in the morning at the mosque.'

'He did not say anything about this. I do not think he believes this is a trend. He says we saw trends in 2003 and 2004 of bad things taking us to Gehenna. Now he sees us heading to ...'

'Paradise?'

I laugh. 'Very clever. No. Not to paradise. But certainly to a better place in this world. He talks about how we can make this present life better for everyone.

He says the effort we make is not for ourselves but for the betterment of each other.'

'He sells shirts? He should be a cleric.'

I laugh again. 'It is good you are here today with me. It is good you are able to make me laugh like this. You have had that gift ever since you were a small girl.'

'I make you laugh and you make me think. That is why we are so close.'

'Aha, you see? That is what Malik would say. He would say we are flowers for each other. We brighten up this present life for each other. We make it good to live. Come, let's go up to the roof. Maybe we can get away from the noise of these children.'

I wonder if Malik will ever tire of the roof, overcome his fear of closed spaces and stop his fretting. He spends so much time up here thinking and worrying. But I know he watches and waits like one of our ancient prophets who paced their rooftops for signs from the stars and portents from the sun. But up here in the midday glare and the oven blast of heat, the rooftop takes our breath away as we adjust our eyes to the sunlight. The breeze is just starting to stir. In an hour the flags across the city will be snapping as the heated air furnaces and beats us down. For the moment the smudge of grey smoke marking the mosque still hangs over the suburbs, fed by a thin column of roiling smoke. Something still burns and the dark memorial to the dead rises to the sky.

We stand side by side with our arms around each other's shoulders, just as we have on so many days. Then

without any words we wander to the other side of the
roof, turning our backs on the rising smoke to look across
other rooftops and imagine an unstained city in which
we can all live without fear of random and twisted and
sudden and violent death.

23

Aadil

You cross your legs too much. That tells me you are uncomfortable. Maybe it is the chair. Maybe the shouts from the other cells. Or is it the fridge-cold air that seeps down those stairs?

It is me? Ha, you are like one of my children who wants something by telling me how much they love me first before they seek a favour or treat. My shouting unsettles you? Shouting? How can I not shout? We have whispered the story so far just to be safe, but now how can I not shout and scream?

Saleh said the rumours he was hearing boasted of a three-call trigger! I did not shout then but in this cell I know I am as good as dead, so why not shout now? Do you know how angry I was? Now I was no different from any other criminal. I knew I had been deceived. But in my heart of hearts I knew I had deceived myself. I could not shout then. You should understand I want to shout now.

As I walked away from Saleh, I struggled to control my breathing, and tears stung my eyes. I stumbled back to my house and must have looked like a man who had lost his mind, falling all over the place and muttering to himself. No matter that I tried hard to behave, just in case they were watching me, I must have seemed out of control. I wept my rage. Killing people at the mosque with the devices I had built. Saleh had said 'three calls' not 'call'. How dare they? How dare they? My head hammered with thoughts of revenge.

Then I knew what I had to do. Just as soon as my head had cooled down. It would not do to make a mistake now. Could I cry out to Allah? Would He hear me? Would He forgive my stupidity? Some say He would. Most say He would judge me for my stupidity. God the judge, not God the merciful. I had helped kill innocent believers. How did I atone for this with Him? There was one answer and that was to stop these men. But to stop them was to kill myself, if I was not careful.

I had to make sure everything I did was invisible to those who surely would be watching me. Betraying Mohammed was something to be done with extreme caution, if I was to not put my family in danger or have retribution visited on any of the students for sins not of their making.

The American checkpoint is a dangerous place. Young men stand alert and ready to shoot. Each checkpoint is different but there are some principles that apply to every

post that is well designed. Firstly, they have to convey a
sense of authority, and if possible they should intimidate
the driver. When you approach a checkpoint there should
be no doubt in your mind that any stupid action will end
in one sorry outcome. All other principles flow from this.
Secondly, you cannot drive through a checkpoint in a
straight line. There is every contrivance to ensure the
driver has to stop and start a number of times. Thirdly,
vehicles are separated from pedestrians. Pedestrians
can be used to distract the search of vehicles. So each
is challenged, inspected, searched and tested but not in
proximity to the other. Fourthly, the supervisors need to
cycle their staff through a checkpoint as often as possible.
That stops the guards from getting bored. They need to
be alert and assertive. The downside to this principle is
that by rotating the guard it is difficult to get to know the
regular traffic or to develop a sense of normality which,
in turn, helps them tune into the abnormal. That is a
small price to pay, however.

To reinforce the intimidation, heavy machine guns are
directed at each vehicle. Many are rapid-fire Gatling guns
mounted in the turrets of armoured personnel carriers.
In some cases a main battle tank will frown down on
a checkpoint with its 120-millimetre cannon. The
Americans are not afraid to use that thing against soft-
skin vehicles and human targets. And then overhead are
the unseen helicopters, drones and aircraft that can be
called in to support a checkpoint if there is any trouble.
It is a place where you speak directly, obey instructions

and keep hands visible at all times. It is best to have an empty car as you travel through.

A checkpoint is the one place I can think of where I might be able to communicate with the Americans. And communicating with the Americans is the only way I can keep myself safe from the deadly hands of Mohammed.

I had considered speaking with Tawfik and asking him to communicate with the Americans through his Ministry. But to have my message go through the Ministry might have left it too late for me and could place Tawfik in danger. Eventually I dismissed the idea. I needed a direct line to the forces on the ground. On the other hand, approaching the Americans directly could get me killed, if Mohammed suspected anything, and my family would die in some horrible way only we Arabs can invent. So it was to be the checkpoint. But very carefully.

A week after my meeting with Saleh I drove slowly into the concrete, sandbagged channel that led to a checkpoint bay close to the International Zone. It is a sensitive area so the soldiers here were on high alert. Machine guns in protected bunkers pointed at me. The control point was still a long way off and I guessed I was being examined in that room by video. Soon a green light came on and a steel barrier in front of my car sank into the ground with a clunk. I was asked to roll forward. All around me were warning signs about carrying weapons in the car, about travelling too fast, about the security people who would shoot to kill if they thought you were a threat. Do you know what these checkpoints are like?

Once you volunteer to enter this maze there is only one way out and that is forward, and it is forward under someone else's command. It is not quite demeaning, for I understand the need for these precautions. But here is one human manipulating another, all the while expecting the worst from him. Vehicles are separated from each other by some distance, the layout of the checkpoint intending to minimise collateral damage from any vehicle bombs.

I drove forward slowly, just letting the car advance with no acceleration. My window was wound down and my hands were draped in full sight over the top of the steering wheel. A soldier in camouflage uniform and dark glasses, body armour and helmet waved me on. To his left-hand side, there were three more soldiers behind a machine gun, watching. Other soldiers were inside a bunker talking on phones or simply sheltering from the sun. I rolled to a stop and a soldier emerged from the bunker. He asked for my identification documents.

This was the moment. 'I am a former colonel in the Republican Guard,' I said, picking the documents up from the passenger seat – it can be lethal to reach inside a jacket for them – and passing them over. In the same smooth movement I slipped to him a small envelope. It was not sealed. 'Please take care,' I said, keeping my eyes straight ahead. 'I need to have this envelope handed to a security specialist. It tells something about what I know of improvised explosive devices. I will come back through here for the next three days until someone is able to give me some instructions about what to do next. But it is dangerous to be talking to you and dangerous to come through here every day. This is not my usual routine. Do you understand?' I was not imperious. I was polite. And I was firm.

The soldier was polite in return. 'I understand, sir. We have your number plates. We will have a response for you tomorrow. Oh, and sir, we will have the right people speak to you. You are not the only one to have made this request.'

With that he handed my identification documents back to me. He had done a good job of gazing at my card while speaking over the top of it and never looking at me. If I was being watched by Mohammed or any of his cronies nothing would have appeared unusual. The soldier waved me forward and flapped his hand at the soldier standing to the front of my car to move aside.

'Just stay driving slowly through here, sir. We want to see you back tomorrow.'

I eased the car forward. As I negotiated around the tall concrete barriers, which completely blocked the checkpoint from the view of the surrounding suburbs, I could feel myself shaking and sweating. This was more precarious than I had imagined it would be. Yet I should have been relieved and I think I was. Others had done the same thing before me. No wonder the soldier was so unfazed about my request and my envelope.

In the envelope, along with a brief outline of what I knew, I had placed one of my old army rank slides. I thought it would help them believe what I said about my rank. I was not about to hand over my name in case the security forces were compromised. But I had asked that whoever met with me should come with that rank slide. Yes, there are many replicas you can purchase but I thought this might be one small way I could confirm they were taking me seriously.

As I continued into the city to buy more electronic parts, my confidence rose. I congratulated myself again for choosing to learn English instead of French when the army gave me the choice. For engineering, English had made sense. Now for my safety I thanked Allah for guiding me down that path.

That evening I sat in the café and spoke again to Saleh who was not so pleased to see me there, I think. I did not sit at the counter as I had done previously, for we were perhaps seen too much together. We did not have a long conversation. All I wanted from him was an address. As he came to deliver the coffee and dates I had not ordered, I asked him for it.

'Thank you, my friend. This coffee is good. When you give me the change please include the address of the man we were speaking about. You will be safe.'

He nodded but looked uneasy. Who was I to promise anyone safety in this town? It was as shallow a promise as anyone could ever make. By it I meant to convey I intended no harm to come to him or his family or his café. Another unspoken language told him we were all in positions where we could guarantee nothing. But this man had trusted his judgment before and decided I was a decent being. It was a big risk he was taking and I could see in his eyes he was not convinced it was the safest choice he had made. He had to believe in the teacher in me, not the designer of electronics for a madman who killed for pleasure and revenge and just because he could.

When Saleh returned he handed me a bundle of change in old and worn bills. I shuffled them into my pocket and paid them no attention until I got home. On my office desk I carefully fanned out the notes and searched for the scrap of paper I expected would have the information I requested. There was none and for a moment my stomach lurched and I felt a hot prickle of panic on my brow. I checked again and turned each note over in case his slip of paper was stuck there. Improbable, but I began to worry that I had dropped something which would compromise me. I feared Saleh might have been working for my enemy, after all. Or for someone else unseen.

I sat back in my chair, puzzled. Saleh was obviously a smart man with lots of experience working for our government in the past. He knew how to protect himself. Why would there be no information? Maybe he did not trust me after all, but I found that hard to believe, given what he had said – and the fact that he had offered up what he had. He did not have to put his life on the line. After all, an officer in the security service ... aha, I thought, the security service. I nearly laughed out loud. He would never write something on a blank piece of paper. I was the stupid one, not Saleh.

Gathering up the soft notes I took myself to the bedroom and examined each of them for any pencil marks. There was nothing. I turned out the room light and switched on the bed lamp, holding the notes to the hot glass. The first three notes revealed nothing except small stains. Fruit juice would make stains like that. The fourth one slowly revealed brown script, written with the care of an artisan and concealed in the brown designs of the note. A number and a street name. No, wait, let's see … two numbers and two street names.

I sighed in relief. Saleh's security credentials were loud and clear in the way he had handled this information. Not only did he use some fruit juice to hide this address but he knew the two real addresses of this man. One where he would live with his family and inside which he would conduct a normal and respectable life. And the second where he would carry out his business. This would be well hidden and well defended and surrounded by a labyrinth of access and exit routes. Sympathisers and supporters, but also any number of innocents, would provide a human shield for him to hide behind. I memorised the details and burned the notes. I would only place those details on paper again once I was at the checkpoint and ready to hand them over.

24

Aadil

I had driven through many roadblocks and barricades in my time but these big concrete checkpoints placed at key sites around the city were not so familiar to me. I had to pass through one on the way to the airport, though that was a visit I had not made for more than two years now. Nonetheless, I had learned to approach them with care and made every effort to ensure there was no reason the edgy soldiers could imagine I was a threat. I never wore sunglasses here. I never carried anything in the car. I had even taken the tinting off the side windows. The car was warmer as a result but in front of these young soldiers it was a safer vehicle.

The day after I dropped off the envelope I drove through the checkpoint again. They were waiting for me as they promised. They walked around the vehicle and a sergeant inspected my documents. I had rarely seen a sergeant here before. And he was a headquarters sergeant.

His boots were not covered with dust and he had the look of a man who was accustomed to air-conditioning. He was not the weary and frazzled guard, attentive yet slow-moving in the heat. This man was sharp and I could see he was looking for someone. Me. He was careful and raised his eyebrows at me over the top of the documents I handed him. It was a question.

'Nothing,' I replied. 'But do you have any news for me?'

He kept looking, eyebrows stuck up in his forehead.

I persisted. 'It has to be soon. And I have to know any transfer here is safe.'

He nodded and handed me back my documents and waved me on.

I watched him in my rear-view mirror as he motioned the vehicle behind me to a stop and an arm reached out of the window to hand over papers. I was assured by this. A soldier who emerged to examine only me would raise suspicion if Mohammed was tailing me. It was important there was no special treatment given to me or my car.

Over the next week I visited the stores beyond the checkpoints three times, buying stock for the classroom. I was using more money than I should have, but it was insurance too. If my attempt to contact the Americans went wrong and I was killed by Mohammed and his lethal friends, I reasoned, then the boys should get as much as I could equip them with to keep their lessons going.

I needed also to learn whatever I could of the American routines and by the time I transited for the final time I was confident the sergeant who checked my credentials would be there for most of the day. I was happy that it was the sergeant and not a new private. The sergeant would hopefully have enough experience to handle me properly when the time came to pass over my information. Yet other things unsettled me. Somehow they knew my car was coming. Did they know where I lived? Were they watching me from the sky, unheard, unseen? Or perhaps my plates were detected by a camera I could not see and the checkpoint alerted that I was on my way?

In the end it did not really matter. I had resolved to do what I was going to do. But today I wanted to arrive when there was a lot of traffic. That way the car had to travel more slowly than usual, allowing me time to write my message as the car rolled forward. I could not commit anything to paper until the last minute in case Mohammed became suspicious for any reason and searched me. Or my car. I had to take every precaution, not for myself but for my family. Imagine what would happen if I had an accident and was killed in a car wreck. Maybe the wrong people would find my notes and my family would be discovered floating down the Tigris. In pieces. With eyes dissolved by acid or throats scorched by petrol. Genitals removed and bones broken. Death would not be easy and no honour of burial given them. Do you understand how on edge I was? How my stomach twisted in fear and I struggled to remain calm.

Self-control in Baghdad is not refraining from eating too much chocolate. Self-control is clamping down the shriek of fear wanting to erupt out of your soul and to engulf you as you strive to do the best for your family and this country. Self-control is talking to the enemy and trusting that your foe will do the right and safe and proper thing by your family. And by you. Self-control is being able to see who the enemy is in the blinding moral sandstorm of this place.

As I entered the final approach leading to the checkpoint, I carefully took my notebook from my inside jacket pocket, placed it on my lap, then slipped seven different Iraqi dinars from out of it. Borrowing Saleh's idea of using the notes, I had thought through every movement. I didn't want to appear to reach for something out of sight. Nor could I look like I was writing or focusing on my lap too much. Anything which in that moment alerted my employer to behaviour out of the ordinary could be my death. Anything after the event that seemed out of the ordinary could also be my death. You see, my employer was not just the hunter. He was the hunted. He knew he was breaking the law. Only a man who breaks the law and knows the penalty is death can understand how alert that makes the senses. The hunted is hyper-vigilant. He sees things he is barely aware he is seeing. He feels things he is not aware he is sensing. He stays alive by his wits, by instinct and by his senses. And he lives because he has learned to heed every signal and transmission and wavelength distortion in his body and mind. He is not on the edge. He is so far over the edge he floats in a sea of suspended consequences. He floats until a ripple warns him away forever or kills him.

I would give him no such ripple. No warning. No vague uneasy feeling he had been betrayed by something he was not able to quantify but which he knew with certainty nonetheless. I looked around and ahead as any bored driver might do as he crawled towards the checkpoint. But as I did so, I was writing hurriedly on each dinar that now sat out of sight on the notebook on my lap. My English handwriting is too easily identifiable – it is a rough scrawl. My Arabic is nondescript and could be written by any person. The first was a 25,000 dinar note. It was an expensive way to signify the importance of the man whose name I wrote beside the picture of the Kurdish farmer. On the two 1000 dinar notes, beside the image of the Baghdad university, I scribbled the addresses of his residences. I hoped the sergeant would see the connection. There were six other addresses Saleh had subsequently slipped me and these I wrote on the 50 dinar notes. Each address was the residence of a supplier of electronics. Were these part of his network? Let the Americans discern who was guilty and who was not.

A soldier's hand was raised and the sergeant approached. I spoke as he came forward. I did not look at him to start with but raised my voice as I reached for my documents.

'I have a name and his two addresses. Also some of his network. You will understand the connections to the notes when I hand them to you.'

He did not respond but held out his hand for my documents just as he always did. I was slightly slower than usual. It allowed me to warn him. 'You need to take the notes in my document. If you cannot I will come back tomorrow.'

His response was simply to flap his hand at me in an impatient gesture. Again I was relieved that he knew what he was doing. Nothing I said was going to allow him to break what must look like a routine inspection. It could have been all too possible to have encountered an enthusiastic amateur who would have been my undoing.

He checked my documents, pulled a pencil from behind his ear, leaned over and made a note on a pad he had hanging at his side, straightened and handed me back my papers. Then he waved me on. The money was gone. For the moment, at least, it was over.

25

Malik

My name is Malik and some days are very good. Some days are so good I know we are going to emerge from this dark night and soon. For I see the steel grey of the dawn and hear the birds stirring and the breeze shifting and can hear the calls of the merchants and the songs of the imams calling us to prayer. I can feel the sands under my feet lifting and old civilisations becoming new. I hear the sound of running feet, bare on the earth, and nowhere is the sound of the high-speed turbines of war. And I smell the scent of roses as they move about us, learning again harmony and peace and goodwill which we will show all our brothers and sisters.

Today is not one of those days.

Today Fatimah is dead. Young and laughing and full of potential. Now all that promise lies trapped in a body wrapped and bound in an ambulance. There is no siren on the ambulance, for the siren is a sound of fragile hope that a life might be saved. Fatimah is beyond a siren and the van drives slowly through the crowds to the hospital. Saleema does not know yet. Only I know, for in this large city I should be so unfortunate as to be walking in my favourite market lane where the merchants have lined the front of their shops with flower boxes, and marigolds struggle in the heat but add their colour and pungent scent to the scene. I know many of the merchants well and enjoy being able to wander and talk to them at leisure. This morning I was there looking for picture frames for my shop. This morning a small bomb exploded in a bicycle rack in the area near me. Three people were wounded and one person was killed. There was a barely audible crack, then the smell of explosive that burns your throat and stings your eyes. The crowd shouted in anger but soon went back to its business. There are too many small incidents like this. This will not make the papers.

What is this about? Why attack like this? Who is the target? Just innocent people. It makes me boil and dangerously angry – I want to go out and do something crazy.

I knew it was dangerous to go near the bomb site in case another one was waiting for the curious. But I needed to see what madness this is and that is when I saw Fatimah, caught in the railing of a small garden, her brown skin honey against the grey soot of this city and her smile frozen in sarcastic accusation at the cradle of her death. I could do nothing except kneel at her side and weep until the ambulance officer pulled me away.

They loaded Fatimah onto a stretcher and treated her respectfully. I thanked them and gave them my name and number. They drove away quietly and the crowd and city closed in behind them and they were gone from sight. And soon from memory. An old man came to straighten the bikes. Two of his friends appeared with a bucket of water and the blood was washed from the street. Soon there was nothing to suggest it had happened. Only I, sitting there in shock, was the single witness to her flight from this earth. Others saw the explosion too, but they did not know her name to mourn her passing. What they do know is that the most powerful antidote to this poison is to continue to live life as best they can. So they move on. They are sorry and sad too, but they know they must keep moving. They know they must maintain the rhythm and embrace it, because the moment they cannot feel the pulse of the city they know they too are dead.

I sit for longer than I should. But what can I do? Have I hoped for too much? Have I clung like a fool to the ideal that we can be better? Should I keep my boy at home and not let him listen to the good man who is teaching him how to be a good man? I know I cannot do that. I know I have to believe in men like Aadil and hope this country can be rebuilt by them, men who will not let this madness continue. I stand up in the crowd. Some people gently acknowledge me and an old woman comes over from her stall and hands me a pomegranate. I smile back weakly and the voice of the imam rattles in my head and makes me sadder.

I hold the fruit of paradise in my hand. But something of paradise should be here for Fatimah too. Where is paradise for her? The tears flow and I cannot stop them. The crowd swirls around a man holding a pomegranate which weighs down his soul and makes him wonder if he can believe. This is no sign for a people who believe. A wet stain on the pavement that will dry to black and eventually vanish among too many stains like it which have also faded from red to black. What memorial will she have as they all cycle and push past here? Who are we that we should walk here in the image of God and hope that we are recognised by our fellows as believers? We presume too much, it would seem, for man is allowed by God to strike us down.

I am jolted by that thought and regret it. This is not God. I am thinking crazy thoughts again. I brush my eyes and use a silk cloth to wipe my face. My eyes are soon able to see again. I gaze at the fruit in my hand and think of the kind person who gave it to me. I look up and see her regarding me. She has been watching the whole time, no doubt willing me to come back, to move on and to feel the pulse again. I smile at her and take a step forward.

Then, in a final glance in honour of where Fatimah was slain, I turn and look at the bicycle rack. A small spatter of dark streaks radiating out like a star from a clear, unmarked centre scores the ground beside the wet, washed pavement drying to black. On top is a tangled piece of electronic hardware I had not seen before. It is bent out of shape and charred. Short wires loop out of it, grasping into the air. I gaze at it and wonder who might have made such a thing of evil.

Then I turn and walk to my shop. I walk away from that black star and lose myself in the crowd. The sandals of others slap alongside me, the chorus of voices and laughter and children shouting and prices being haggled pick me up and bear me along. Without knowing, they all lay down their flowers around me and in their pulse I become human again and dare to hope that we can all love again.

I am home early. The traffic was thick and slow but I did not really care. My stomach is sick and I feel sad. How can we think we are rebuilding ourselves when we see beautiful people like Fatimah killed in such a casual way? What am I going to tell Saleema? How can I tell her? I am glad when I arrive home that she is not there. The children are not there. The guard tells me they are at the park at the end of the street with three other families and the puppies. That they are down there makes me nervous, but I force myself to leave them alone and go inside. I splash cold water on my face and change my shirt for a loose one with no collar. Then I go up onto the roof.

I look into the hot bronze sky and see and hear nothing. There are no helicopters. Only when I turn around do I notice the white blimp in the haze. It has been hanging tethered over the city for so long now. No one really knows what it does. Some think it has powerful cameras watching the city. Some think it is for communications. Others think it has radars inside detecting where any mortars or artillery rounds are fired from. Maybe it is all these things. I care not to think about it today and turn back to the view of palms and rooftops and aerials and Iraqi flags snapping in the hot wind. These are the things I want to be normal in my city. I don't want a foreign white blimp hanging over us, even if it is keeping us safe. I want Fatimah back. I do not want to have to deliver news like this to my wife, who is down near those eucalypt trees somewhere, being carefree with neighbours and children and puppies. Children and dogs. They go together and it is a picture that relieves my unhappiness. I go to the chair and sit down. Soon I am asleep.

When I wake up I am drowning in rivers of sweat. The sun is setting and the sky is soft and has lost the brittle look it gets when it has been baked too long by our desert sun. Saleema is standing at the door, looking at me and shaking her head.

'You crazy Iraqi,' she jokes, 'sleeping up here in the heat. Look at you, melting away into the Tigris.'

I wipe myself dry with the towels that hang on the line along the side of the house. 'Yes, very crazy. I must have worn myself out with the shop to fall asleep up here.'

'I am thinking something must be wrong for you to be home early from the shop. In these last weeks you are home early only if something is wrong.'

With a start I think – 'Fatimah' – and Saleema must see my face react.

'There is something wrong. I can see it.' She comes over and places her hands on my head, pausing for a moment to look at me before perching beside me. 'You can't tell me?'

'I don't want to tell you. Someone has died.'

The fabric across her back suddenly goes taut and her shoulders square. From behind I can see she is waiting for the news. I cannot tell her straight away. I want to but cannot. The silence seems to go on forever and finally I have to say her name.

'It is Fatimah.'

For just a few heartbeats she stays rigid, looking straight across the roof to the setting sun and seeing nothing. Then she slowly collapses forward off the recliner onto the concrete of the roof and bursts into sobs. She does not let me help her. She is in her own grief. I have to let her stay there until she has run out of tears, tears that melt away into the Tigris.

I wait until the sun goes down. She has stopped moving. The cook is looking after the children. Saleema has sobbed then gone quiet, then sobbed long, wrenching cries before falling silent again. She is still at my feet, embracing the concrete. Mourning in the dust and ashes of a country that has been on fire for too long and has rained its ashes on our roof and now on the heart of my Saleema. So long in this latest conflict we have been without the violence touching any of us closely that we were the minority. In a country of majorities and minorities we were the small few who had had no direct wounding. Scorched maybe. But today the fragments of this madness and evil splinter into us and we have become wounded.

The hot breeze tugs and pulls at us and dries our tears as they fall on our cheeks and into the dust. It is time. I reach down and touch Saleema on the waist. She is soft and limp, as if asleep. But she stirs and stands and gazes into the velvet-evening blue-black darkness. Tonight the helicopter phantoms beat over us, become silent, then come throbbing back. There are no lights. Something is happening in the city, through its streets, across its shadowy houses. I can hear the whine of tank turbines. And the rumble of tyres on armoured personnel carriers as they chase the turbines. Every now and then a shout from a soldier or tank commander. Is it exercises? Is it the beginning of a new madness? Is Fatimah the portent of something terrible returning? Can we stand to see our fellow men floating down the Tigris again? Cut down by former neighbours and friends? I take Saleema in my arms and hold her. She leans in and places her weight on me and whispers her fears, echoing mine.

'These are the sounds of war. We have heard them before.'

'We have heard them before. But it is too hard to know if there will be any fighting. They might be training.'

She shakes her head. Her heart is broken. Everything now will be coloured by Fatimah, and in her mind we are at war. It is going to be difficult to have the boy attend class. I will talk to her about that later.

I go down the stairs to get Saleema a drink. There on the table is the ruby-red and emerald-green pomegranate given to me by the woman at the market. It crosses my mind to give it to Saleema, but now is not the time to bother her with small comforts. She needs to weep her tears and listen to her sorrow. Taking the fruit in my hands I feel its firm ripeness, its promise of life and sustenance. Its pulse of life. Somehow it gives me resolve and I decide two things. The first is that Imaad will go to school. What is the use of a life that is cowed and beaten? The second is that he should give this fruit to the teacher working so hard for his education and that of all the boys in his class. The fruit of paradise should go to a man who is trying to make a paradise real for us here.

26

Aadil

You look as relieved as I felt. It was over, yes, but here I am in prison. Jailed like a common criminal and locked away to rot or even die, I should imagine. It was over, all right. But it was the beginning of the end for me. You should not put your pencil away – there is more to tell.

A week had passed since I went through the checkpoint and nothing had happened that was so unusual that I should be immediately concerned for my family. Or myself. But there were ripples that were getting my attention. The boys started to trickle back to the classroom. A ripe pomegranate sat on my desk, turning a deep ruby red and its leathery skin splitting open, spilling its translucent baby gems onto my desk. The boys eyed it expectantly. The son of the shirt-seller had pressed it into my hands and said his father insisted only a good man should eat this fruit, for it came from a market in which a family member had died. Is God speaking to me? Does

He speak outside the Book? First Saleh. Now the shirt-seller whose boy sits in the front row and feeds off every gesture, every word from me. Are these men modern prophets? How can that be? Are these times in which we behave like filthy swine when prophets need to be sent to warn us? I did not know what would happen, or if the message was clear. Or if I was safe.

As I said, if a man is breaking the law, or is even being hunted by the law, he is extremely aware of all that is happening around him. He is alert to subtle changes. Things out of the ordinary. Some days ago, a police and army patrol went through our neighbourhood. They were all Iraqi men but had one American adviser. Such patrols are becoming common in Iraq. But I had never seen a patrol in my lanes before. Mine was not a war-zone suburb. Why, just after I had been through the checkpoint, had a patrol gone through? Were they looking for me, setting me up, getting ready to confront or save me? In Iraq there are no clear lines. The man you imagine is your saviour could be your death. Or the man whom you fear for your life can whisper a warning and deliver you from the snare.

After the patrol, a strange fellow set up a stall on the corner of the street. Who does that? He sold everything and nothing. Postcards and batteries. Soda drinks and chocolate bars. Fake military ranks from the US Civil War, plastic Russian rank badges. Small wooden souvenir cases with 'Iraq' engraved on their lids. And numerous cigarettes. He did well. It might not have bothered me, but postcards? Who in the depths of Baghdad would buy poorly printed postcards and where would he send them? It made me suspicious.

I was suspicious also of the men who were now in the street outside the school. They looked scruffy and out of place, and I did not feel they were Americans, which left me only one other choice. Was Mohammed casing me or was I the attention of someone else? I could not allow myself to think too much about it. Things were now set in motion that I could not alter and I was resigned to going where events took me. I couldn't fret about men in the street I did not know. There were better things to dwell on. Like Tawfik and his success in being selected to go to Europe on a training course. Many countries were helping train our new young diplomats and he was excited to be flying to Italy and France and Germany and England and even to the US for twelve weeks.

He came to my house to discuss it, but with all my children that was not the best place to converse so we walked down to the café. Saleh nodded in recognition and pointed with his chin at a table tucked away in the corner under fake red candles which flickered their weak light intermittently, conveniently cloaking us in shadow. We sat in the evening heat and listened to the helicopters and the birds and barking dogs and shouting, sometimes crying, children.

'I was in trouble in my training today. You will understand how that can be – you are a teacher, after all,' announced Tawfik.

I imagined him in the back row of my class, making life intolerable for me. 'How were you in trouble? Throwing things?'

'No.' He laughed. 'Nothing like that.'

'Well, go on.'

He glanced at me with a puzzled look before speaking. Had I been too curt?

'I said something today that I would not have dared say as a boy. And I hope you are not offended by it either.'

'Try me,' I suggested. 'I think I can hear anything. Not much will surprise me these days.'

'I asked the class – we are a group of fifteen diplomats – I asked the class if there is something not right about the international help we are getting. I think I was saying what everyone was thinking.'

'Go on.'

'I asked the class why it was that no other Arab countries are helping us reconstruct. They might supply money but they do not help. All our neighbours are concentrating on building stronger barriers and borders and fences. Building ways to keep us in and others out. Walls are going up here, when in Europe they have come down. Our neighbours do not help. They cut each other off and they cut us off.'

'Was your question about the help or about the walls?'

'It was about both but mainly it was about the help. Think about it. The few countries training us in our diplomatic skills are non-Arab states. We are doing most of our training in Rome.'

'You have a problem with that?'

'No, not at all. I am looking forward to it. We fly out next week, to Amman and then to Rome. But why is it that the countries building us are not our Muslim brothers?'

'And you are surprised this question got a reaction?'

'No. But here is the thing. We had just been discussing our new freedoms with a friend who owns a coffee shop. We were complaining we had no freedoms with the Americans here. He is a wise old man. He said we might not have freedom to move around the country but we now have freedom of our mind and freedom of our mouth. We can say what we think. Mainly. If you are on the wrong side of a religious faction, you still need to keep your mouth shut. But we are now free to say things we were not free to say before. Our coffee merchant thinks this is the beginning of true freedom.'

'So what was the relevance of this conversation?'

'We had this conversation on the pavement with an old sage who is a clever man and gives us good training of our minds. We all agreed that what I said was true. Then when I was back in class and suggested our real friends were those who helped us, not those who wanted to build walls around us, the class turned into a cauldron. Not everyone has had the benefit of our informal education at the feet of the coffee merchant.'

'And your teacher?'

'The teacher was in shock. He did not know what to say.'

'He is surprised that you said this?'

'No, he was disappointed that we could not debate this point in a diplomats' training course!'

'But I have not heard anything in what you said that is truly provocative. Is that all you said?'

He looked at me and grinned a wide, open and friendly grin. He was going to make a good representative of Iraq just on handsome looks alone. 'You know me too well, uncle. Far too well.'

'And?'

'I asked my fellows if it was true that Iraq remembered its friends. That we are true to our friends and never forget those who have helped us, and never forgive those who have wronged us. They agreed these were our strengths and our weaknesses. But I wanted them to concentrate on those who we counted as friends because they helped us.

'Then I suggested we should never forget the Christian states that are helping us. Italy. France. England. Norway. Even Australia. These are people helping us. Not our neighbours.'

'And you want to be a diplomat?'

He shifted uneasily. 'I was less interested in the specific thought and more interested in the idea that we could now be free to think and feel and say things that are real without fear of the police or the military or the clergy.'

'We will always have to fear the clergy, no matter how free we finally become. But what you said was a ridiculous thing right now. Soldiers from a Christian country patrol our streets. They created this terror in the first place.'

'Yes, they might have. But have you met one who has not wanted to go home? We know they are doing their job and want out of here.'

'They kill just like the rest of the cowards around here.' Suddenly I was rationalising what I had been doing with the triggers. But nothing was going to allow me to do that with integrity anymore. I could not speak and stared at the floor lest I betray myself. It would be easy to dash myself on the rocks of this young man's ideals.

'You are all right?'

'Yes, I am fine. I am just thinking of how mad this place is. Americans liberate us, get confused, then oppress us. Other Americans behave like friends and help us rebuild infrastructure their colleagues have smashed. Who are friends? Who are enemies? Who are we that eat our young? Or cook them at least?'

He nodded. 'We have all heard that and other stories. We are people who simply have to remember our friends, be friends and make sure we create a country that has no walls around it.'

'Ah, the diplomat speaking.'

'But it is true.'

'It is true. Very true.'

We finished our coffee and sat in silence for a while, listening to the sounds of the night, then rose and wandered back to the house.

As I lay on my bed that night it was difficult to sleep. How could I sleep when I thought of those triggers being used for unholy acts of war? How could I sleep when people were watching me and I did not know who they were? And how could I sleep when I perceived a man out there who may have discovered I had betrayed him? It made me have bad dreams and I woke in hot blood many times that night.

27

Malik

This is a bitter time for us. Yesterday, in the morning, I said my son must go to school. It is a token effort to be strong. To instil hope in my family for a future. But I stayed home to be with Saleema and to take her early to Fatimah's grandparents, Fatimah's home since she lost her family. What a cup of sorrow they are forced to draw from. They did not weep but that will come. They silently embraced us and welcomed us in for refreshments. They were too broken to speak and we left after a polite interval. We will share our stories at another time.

Today Saleema pats me on the arm. 'Go to the shop. I will be okay. You do not need to hover,' she says.

It does not feel right, but after she gently pushes me to the door I go. I drive slowly to work. There are no signs of war; there are only the signs of people ready for war. Saleema can relax. The noises she heard the night Fatimah was dead were the noises of training.

I do not open my shop but sit with Mahrus and the boys, who are nearly ready to leave the country on a course they are taking abroad. Diplomats. Mahrus knows my sorrow. He guesses at Saleema's sorrow. The young men know nothing.

'You have not opened the shop today – or yesterday. It is just as well I now have all my shirts,' one of them teases.

I smile at him and sip some coffee, which Mahrus has pushed into my hand. 'I can open it, if you like. Good shirts are still for sale in the best shop on this side of the bridge.'

'You are okay, Mr Malik?' inquires another. 'You are not happy today. Every day is a good day, I hear you say. You do not look like you believe that today.'

'Today is a good day,' I whisper. 'But yesterday was a bad day. And the day before that. That day a beautiful woman, a niece of my wife, was killed in a small explosion not far from here. I saw it happen. She was my family too. It is hard to feel good today. But I know it is a good day.' I force a smile onto my face.

The young men stare at the ground and say nothing. Most of them would have lost family and friends. I know I am being respected by people who know this pain. After we have drunk our coffee in silence, one of them, with his elbows on his knees and still gazing at the pavement, speaks. He speaks of the hope he has for the future. And he speaks of the people he knows. And he speaks of a man who used to be in the army but now teaches boys at a school that cannot pay him. That, said the young man, is the hope of this country. I have to agree.

The phone in my house does not ring often. When its old bells jangle on the wall I am startled. People who know me call my cell phone. Saleema and I look at each other until it rings off. For a few seconds there is the sound of the breeze stirring the bushes at our front gate, and the scrape of hanging palm fronds doodling in the dust with their dry and withered tips. Then the phone rings again. It is insistent and urgent and official so I pick it up.

'Hello?'

'Mr Malik Abdullah?'

'Yes.'

'You left a number with an ambulance driver following a bombing some days ago.'

'Yes. You're calling about that?'

'Yes. We have been trying to call the number you left, but you know how unreliable the networks have been. I am glad to have found you.'

'Yes. Who is this?'

'Ah, this is Sergeant Habib. Are you able to identify this person? You would help us if you could do so.'

'I understand. Yes. We have been hoping to retrieve my niece's body. We have been waiting for someone to contact us.'

'Indeed, she should have been buried. We would have arranged for that, except you had left your number.'

'Where should I go?'

'To the morgue at the general hospital.'

'When should I do that?'

'Any time of the day is okay, but please if it can be tomorrow, that would be good.'

'I can tell you over the phone who she is.'

'I am sure you can. But we need a physical identification and you cannot do that over the phone.'

I tell the sergeant I will be there first thing in the morning and hang up. Saleema is looking at me with tear-stained eyes and puffy cheeks. So sad. But she is clear in her voice when she speaks to me.

'You go to the shop. I will go to the hospital. It is the least I can do for my niece, my precious sister.'

'You cannot go down there. It is not safe. Besides, it will take you two hours or more to walk there.'

'I can walk. And I can go with Rashida. She's a neighbour who knew Fatimah well.' She wraps up her shawl as she speaks and I know any discussion is at an end. Even if I did drive to the hospital she and her friend would still walk there to pay their respects.

28

Aadil

You are early for the interview today. Why is that? Have you found my family? No, I thought not. They are dead, you know.

I know that. You think I am still held here with no medical attention all these days and my family has not been found? Mohammed and his sick men would have killed them. I am dead too. So answer me, why are you early?

You shrug. That is not a good sign. You are a journalist investigating things and you do not investigate your own mind? I think not. I think you know. You want to know what has happened at the checkpoints, no?

Perhaps. Ah, perhaps yes, perhaps no. You do not convince me. Perhaps you want to know how the checkpoint message went wrong, how it was that I was betrayed. How I am still trussed up here to be hosed down once a day like a butcher's carcass.

You protest your motives too much. Sit down before I tire of you. Listen and see if there is anything in this you can learn from. I see you have learned not to judge. It is a start. All teachers have to start with small victories with their students. No judgment is my first victory with you.

I had become nervous about the classroom. Now I see too many people I do not know. They stand in the sun and watch the school. They loiter in the heat, sometimes under the shade of an occasional straggling tree, watching the streets. They were never there before I handed over the details on the banknotes. The small stall at the end of the street had me most worried. There had been far too many young men cruising around it. Something was not right. I sensed it. And in Baghdad your senses will save you. But what was I to do? Should I stay in my house and hide? What about my family? What about the students? What about my own soul? Am I a man if I stay at home with the women and children? Am I a coward? And what if they wanted to attack me? I would only put the lives of my family in danger. I thought they were in danger anyway. But how could I think clearly?

Many times I looked out from the classroom and gazed across the yard to see two men on the street, on the other side of the school wall. I caught their eye. They were in no hurry to look away. I tried not to hold their gaze. By now they must have known I knew they were there. How was I to stay safe when I did not know who they were? None of my friends would have had answers. And in Baghdad who are your friends? If I asked a neighbour of twenty years if he knew who the young men were at the stall in my street, I might invite violence on my head because I do not know that he is paid by a gang, or faction, or enemy group. Who is my brother? I no longer knew.

Then the Americans made contact. They told me they were ready to move on the information I had provided and that I should meet with my contact. This time I was less worried about calling a meeting with Halim than I was about how the Americans had communicated with me. Through Saleh, no less. I was dumbfounded. Who was Saleh really? And who was he working for? Was he playing some kind of double game?

I was caught up in a network I could not see or even sense. I could see no beginning, no end. Worse, I had no understanding of what was connected to what. Do you know how an engineer can be unsettled by such abstraction? This was no design project with clear rules. I was trapped in a world over which I had no control, immersed in something so ambiguous I had no knowledge of how to keep safe or move forward or extract myself.

Saleh sent me a strange message. Safe but strange. It came by way of one of the numerous boy messengers that run the lanes of this city. He would be holding a special event at his café tomorrow night. He had bought a new television, one of those flat ones, and would be screening a replay of the World Cup final. Special coffee. Special sweets. I must come. It was such a curious invitation I knew it must indicate something else on his mind. So I didn't wait but went immediately to see him, just as soon as the runner had nodded his thanks and skipped out of sight.

Saleh had news that churned my stomach: I should contact Halim and ask him about the next round of work. Why would I do that when I had never done such a thing before? And what did Saleh know that he should suggest this? Suggest? No, he was insistent and pressed me to have Halim come to the screening of the football match.

What did I do, you ask? What could I have done? I had no choice but to contact Halim. And he replied so very quickly my fear only worsened. I left a Winston packet at my front doorstep overnight. By morning when I left for school, there was a crushed version answering it. The sickness in my stomach worsened. I had felt so close to getting out from under this. Was I too late? What if my covert scribblings on those grubby banknotes had been compromised? Had they discovered my betrayal? Who was Saleh? What did he know? Who paid him and where did his loyalty really lie? I had no idea. Was he in concert with Halim, after all, that he should know so much about him and have Halim reply so rapidly? I fought back my panic. On the way to school I calmed down. Surely if they had found me out, I and my family would be dead. Yet there was too much unusual activity in the street to assure me of anything.

I did not open Halim's crushed packet until I was in the class laboratory and there were no boys around to watch me. We were intending to do a project that day on bones and how they work. Skeletons and things inside a body are endlessly fascinating to boys. Why is that, I wonder? I had prepared some cattle bones the butcher had given me. They were neatly sawn in cross-section, so the matrix of webbed tissue was clearly visible, as was the marrow. I ran my fingers across the skeleton and felt the life in it even though it was dead. How wondrously we are made. How quickly we destroy. How sad I teach about bones using cattle when all the boys in the class have seen more human bones than any child their age should. What am I saying? They have seen more bones than any adult should. Bones from graves. Bones on the street. Bones shattered with clinging clumps of flesh. Grey bones, leaking through scorched and charred flesh.

I countered my own lamentation. Maybe by using cattle bones and showing how God had put thought into our design I could encourage these boys to take care of their bodies and those of their neighbours. Teaching using cattle bones to try and bring back to these students the joy of understanding how cleverly everything is made. I shook myself from these thoughts and looked again at the slip of paper tucked into the cigarette packet.

It told me, in the familiar handwriting of Halim, to meet him at the café as I requested. But the message was unusual because he took the trouble to confirm that we would talk about our next projects. He never left a message except to convey a place and time. Should I be wary of a more conversational tone? What was I to do?

If I did not turn up and I was supposed to be there, I ran the risk of being punished, or my family being hurt. If I did turn up and it was a trap, perhaps that was the best option. I would be punished and my family not. Either way Mohammed would likely know, since his men were all over town watching me. They were here at the school waiting for me again. They were watching me leave the house. They were watching me walk to school. They were everywhere, and when the time came, they would catch me up in their net and I would be powerless to respond. We are trapped by the people we love. Trapped to do predictable things that an enemy can exploit. I hated my weakness but I knew I could do nothing except be honourable. And I could only be honourable if there were things I had done that had been dishonourable. So what was I to do? I hated the answer but was compelled to obey it: I had to go to the café.

That night Saleh started his replay late and Halim was at the café before me. What would you make of that? If you were not a resident of Baghdad, you might think this contact was running early. Or maybe had other business before your business. But no, this was a dangerous sign. This told me he was worried about our security. It told me he was worried about his security because he thought *I* was a threat to his security and he had arrived early in case I had set a trap. Or in case a trap had been set that neither of us knew about but could smell. Either way, if he was worried about his security, then I should be concerned about mine. His ashtray was full. He was smoking and tapping his fingers. There was no comfortable indolence in his face; he was a falcon alert. I caught the eye of Saleh and signalled for coffee before I sat down. Greetings were mumbled and brief. I started straight in.

'You have been here a long time and the hour is late. Is something not right?'

'Long time? What makes you say that?' he spat. I was surprised at his tone. What did he suspect about me?

I tried to stay calm and keep my voice steady. I indicated the ashtray. 'You are never allowed to sit at a table in this café with someone else's dirty ashtray. Those are all yours?'

He paused and seemed to settle in his seat. 'We hired you because you are clever. You are observant as well, I see.'

'You have to be, around this city.'

'Then if you are observant tell me what is different around your life these days.'

Now I was very careful. Some in so-called democratic countries ask, 'Who watches the watchers?', as if this is some moral dilemma. In Iraq we want to know 'Who owns the watchers?', for the answer is not moral but a matter of life. Or death. I paused and looked away and appeared to think before giving him a cautious reply.

As I did so two men drifted in and fussed about their chairs before sitting down at a table with a good view over our shoulders of the soccer game on Saleh's new screen. They seemed engrossed in the television and I did not worry about them but paid attention to Halim. They were not concerned with us.

'There has been a small stall set up at the end of my street. It's out of place. It doesn't seem to do anything except attract a lot of loitering young men. I am uncomfortable about that because my children play in the street. I worry for their safety.' I was not about to admit that I thought they were surveillance and alarm him.

He nodded. 'That is all?'

I paused again. 'Yes, I think so. So much of the city seems to be coming back to the old routines, now the Americans are patrolling into our suburbs and not hiding in their bases. There are more stalls open. The streets are trading again. Yet it is hard to know what is now routine and what is displaced. It makes staying alert all the more difficult.'

'Do you know who owns the new stall?'

I shook my head. 'There is no one who is in or near it that belongs to the neighbourhood.'

He scratched his greying stubble with a thumb while his cigarette, caught between his fingers, rained ash onto the table. He looked troubled and unsettled. I asked the question.

'Something is wrong?'

'We are not sure. There seems to be a lot of new faces around us and, like you, we cannot tell who is friend or foe. And suddenly none of us has any trouble making cell-phone connections. You know how bad getting connections here can be. Over these last days we have had no trouble.'

'That is the same for everyone, no?'

'Not that we can tell. Others still have trouble. Our contacts over in the International Zone tell us they still have trouble making connections.'

I knew what he meant. If the privileged few cannot make a connection then we all suffer the same inconvenience. But if the networks clear up, we know it is because the Americans are tracking something. If you are doing something illegal and relying on the phone, clear networks are a good reason to stop transmitting. Just in case.

'So you think what we have done is being watched?'

He scratched his chin again and looked sideways at me. My stomach turned in knots but I held his gaze and tried to imagine how I would react if I did not have the guilty knowledge of betrayal in my head and in my heart. I blinked.

It was so very fast I barely saw it coming. I had been careful to appraise the two men who had entered earlier but they had not caused me to worry. I was suspicious of them but in the same way I was suspicious of all others, and I thought I was ready to react to trouble from them or anybody else in the café. I was so tuned in to the café I did not see the black shadows race in from the street until it was too late. I was belted across my face with a wooden rod and smashed backwards onto the floor. Halim roared and struck out as he fell, his broken nose gushing fluid and blood, his blazing eyes screaming their rage and hatred and frustration and loathing as his head cracked and bounced off the tiles. His cry mingled with my own scream of pain as my face cracked sideways across the steel feet of the coffee table and my teeth rattled out of my head. Salt filled my mouth and white heat pulsed through my temples. Strobe lights flashed, glass shattered, boots kicked my ribs, a stun grenade cracked and screeched, and the two shadows sitting against the corner pulled weapons before a flurry of popping, muffled shots pushed them down the wall with their spilt coffee and surprised looks. So they were covering Halim's back, after all. But not covering their own.

I got ready to die in the throbbing haze of light and salt and smoke and screams and insane laughter and whooping shouts of adrenaline-shot men dressed in black. I lay still and waited for oblivion and the judgment. I thought of all I had done. What goodness would God find in my life? I readied my mind for Him, to give an answer to Him of all I am and all I have done, for 'It is God who splits the grain and the date-stone, brings forth the living from the dead; He brings forth the dead too from the living.'

Then it all went black.

I woke up in the helicopter. For a moment I wondered what judgment this was. My hands were bound with plastic and were severely cut. I could barely see through swollen eyes. Under the beat of the blades I slept again and woke while being carried into my cell. I heard no voices, just the scraping of boots, the grunt of effort, the heavy breathing of closeness, smelt the hot canvas odour of cloth-trapped sweat, heard the bang of steel. The plastic was cut and my hands throbbed with pulsing pain. My eyes were wiped of their crust though I kept them closed. A hand opened my mouth and I felt a finger in rubber probe inside until it touched the exposed nerves of my jaw. I felt myself falling into a deep, deep hole, saw green lightning flood my head and felt the first moment of soaking warmth in my groin before I hit the bottom and everything was no more.

29

IMMEDIATE

FROM: HQ VCORPS
TO: HQ USCENTCOM

INFO: CJTF-SWA
CENTAF, SHAW AFB
NAVCENT
SOCCENT, MCDILL AFB
CCB
ARCENT, FT MCPHERSON, GE
NSACSS FT GEORGE G MEADE MD
CDR USTRANSCOM SCOTT AFB IL

SECRET
COMMANDER'S REPORT

OPERATION DESCRIPTION
1(S) This report reviews the recent security operation
in Baghdad environs carried out in response to

information provided by a former senior Iraqi military officer (identity confirmed) about improvised explosive device (IED) manufacture. The informant had revealed the source and place of manufacture of the IED trigger devices. The IED manufacturer and his operations have been positively identified by multiple sources. A number of suppliers of electronic components of the triggers were also positively identified by multiple sources. This operation was timed to ensure the head of IED manufacture and his suppliers were all arrested simultaneously. In the lead-up to the arrests an additional protective cordon was placed around both the informant and his family. The informant was arrested in the operation in order to protect his identity and disguise his role from the target.

2(S) The informant was asked to call a meeting with his contact within the organization responsible for the IED manufacture. Communications with the informant were via a previously established military intelligence contact (cross-ref. separate reporting on Operation Chainmail), who owned and operated the café frequented by the informant. The informant advised Chainmail he had previously called for a meeting, even though this was not usual practice. He was worried that, by initiating this meeting out of routine, his contact would be on guard and suspect compromise. He warned that he could not be too specific about when and where lest that make the target suspicious. He was provided a primary time and a back-up time and agreed he needed to ask to meet at his usual café. Our informant agreed to ask for a meeting requesting an understanding of next phases of his work.

3(S) The person responsible for the IED manufacture is a criminal known to local security forces, with suspected links to former Ba'ath Party ministers. He was able to operate with relative impunity and archived records reveal he was feared by the police. Initial evidence links him to police in his employ. Separate investigations are ongoing. His forces were concentrated near the political headquarters of the Iraqi government in and near the International Zone. However, it is believed his IED-led activities have been directed at achieving criminal ends, payback and establishing his own fiefdom. We understand his key strategy was to create a destabilized environment into which he could exert his own influence. He rarely engaged US military forces, the Iraqi army or the national police. He is believed to have attacked the Iraqi police service, when that has served his purpose.

4(S) The target was well protected and preferred to move within the market areas of Baghdad, usually dressed poorly and on foot. Apprehension timing was coordinated for late evening hours (local) with markets closed but his network still socialising. Timing took into account the need to apprehend the informant at the same time as the manufacturer's network. The closely built-up area prevented the use of vehicles in the immediate area of the target's residence, so the insertion of arrest teams by helicopter was required.

5(S) In the lead-up to the arrests, protective surveillance of the informant was provided by the Iraqi national police around his residence and the school where he taught on an itinerant basis. It is highly likely the informant became aware of this surveillance but initial interrogation confirms he was not aware of the authority behind the coverage. The operation was at risk if he assumed the coverage was hostile. To mitigate that risk a more discrete team was in place to intervene if necessary and prevent the informant from precipitating any action of his own. Throughout this operation the informant maintained a normal routine and pattern of behaviour which we do not believe aroused any suspicion in the target or target's forces.

6(S) The informant revealed that the target had a high degree of communications and technology sophistication and discipline. Other sources and pre-operation analysis led us to assess his strength at about seventy-five supporters. The target's personal security detail was armed and comprised seventeen men. The security detail inhabited three safe houses connected to the target's residence. Each security detail member is believed to have been connected to a cell-phone-alert capability. A critical supply network of six suppliers was identified by the informant and is believed to have been on the same alert network. The timing of the arrest meant suppliers, security details and the target all needed to be closely coordinated to ensure one group did not alert another.

7(S) The mission was to arrest the elements which constituted 'high pay-off targets' only, viz. the target, his security personnel, the informant and his intermediary, and the six suppliers. The primary course of action was to have a vehicle and foot cordon in place around the residence of the target as well as a cordon around each of the six suppliers by 0035 hours local time. At 0035 all phone cells in Baghdad central local time were to be off-line until 0045. Arrest teams were inserted on buildings one, three and five. Security teams were inserted in lanes Alpha and Charlie. Tactical air support was employed to cover any escape contingency. A simultaneous operation to arrest the informant and his intermediary, along with any associates accompanying the intermediary, was planned for a separate location.

8(S) All airborne units were in place at 0038 local time. Special forces airborne units were in place but standing off to react to any attempt to break the cordon. Ground units were in place at 0041 due to unexpected traffic congestion. Insertion of units into streets and on rooftops took place at 0041.

9(S) The target was arrested without incident by security team Bravo at or about 0042. Target offered no resistance but his security teams were in the process of being activated as Alpha and Bravo teams approached safe houses. Rooftop team Alpha entered building from rooftop and engaged and killed three personnel who offered resistance. These were the only casualties.

10(S) Five of the six suppliers were arrested without incident and their premises were secured for further examination by Iraqi police service personnel. The sixth supplier was not arrested, as he was not found at his residence. The police do not believe he was alerted and are maintaining surveillance on his premises with a view to arresting him when he returns.

11(S) The informant was detained together with intermediary at Chainmail's café. Both resisted arrest and have received medical treatment. Informant has a broken collarbone and facial injuries. Security forces engaged two personnel who drew weapons when the informant and his intermediary were being apprehended. These may have been bodyguards of the intermediary but their identity and role is yet to be confirmed. Both personnel were killed.

12(S) All detainees, including informant, are located at Camp Cropper. All are being held separately with our informant held in same block as target.

13(S) All detainees were searched prior to transport to Camp Cropper. Target had three cell phones removed from his person. In the course of the morning he was observed making calls from a fourth cell phone. Six calls were logged. An investigation is under way to determine the source of the cell phone.

REMARKS

14(S) This was a successful operation with nil blue-force casualties. However, we believe the target made calls from a smuggled cell phone which have potentially initiated IEDs (ref. following paragraph). This is to be confirmed in subsequent reporting. Target is confused about who has provided information on his operations. Currently we believe informant is not suspected. Informant is being held in proximity to the target to reinforce perception by target of innocence. Suppliers are being accused by the target of being the weak link. Follow-up action required with national police is being reported separately.

15(S) Cursory analysis of IED technologies shows sophistication in design of two trigger types (cross-ref. separate technical-analysis report). Both trigger types can be set with timing delay between receipt of command and initiation of the device. More comprehensive analysis is to be reported separately. Attention is drawn to all military commands that phone calls by target are likely to have commanded IEDs which have yet to detonate. Target debriefing is currently focused on understanding if commands have been sent and, if so, to where. Target is not yet forthcoming on the deployment of his IEDs and trigger. Informant has provided full briefing on his designs and alerted us to the delay function.

16(S) An assessment of the success of the operation is being assisted by naval reservist intelligence officer LT E.D. Peters. Peters is presenting herself to the informant in the role of a journalist and has adopted an effective passive interview approach. The informant is volunteering information consistent with his initial admissions to us. Interviews are recorded and will be forwarded for further analysis. Informant appears to have been truthful to date. His discourse to LT Peters appears to corroborate his claims about who he was working for, his modus operandi, and that he was not employed by any other person.

CLASSIFIED BY: CAPT BRIAN HAMLIN, USA, J3
REASON: 1.4(A)
DECLASSIFY ON: 01 JUN 2013

30

Malik

My name is Malik and I still live in Baghdad. I desperately want today to be a mostly very good day, for I see signs that things are turning for the best. If I can look forward then I can have every day as a good day. Today Saleema will be walking to the morgue with her friend Rashida. I would rather she not walk up to the hospital at all, but she is a stubborn person. Besides, what can I say? Her very best friend is dead, randomly executed in an act scheming and heartless. Who puts a bomb in a bicycle rack? What was the intention of that? Just placed somewhere to inconvenience as many citizens as possible? Maybe it was young boys who have made this bomb, experimenting with things they have heard and read about. My soul is grieved when I think on this, my heart heavy with a black weight of darkness which blankets any hope I have for my fellow believers. How is it that we can climb out of this morass when we kill off the experimentation of

it? When death has become a plaything, we deserve
only the judgment of an angry God. Is He angry? I do
not know. How can I know God? But I hope He is not
yet turning His eye of judgment on us. Too many good
things are happening for me to think He is truly angry at
us, though He has every reason to hate us. We cook our
children alive. We bomb into eternity a beautiful young
woman with the eyes of heaven.

We did not tell the children about Fatimah straight
away. How do you tell them such a terrible thing? We
were cowards, for the children knew there was something
wrong on those days we were silent and their mother
grieved. There was no escaping, of course. The girls
were insistent that Fatimah come and play with them,
wanting to know where she was, and finally Saleema
broke down in the morning as we were getting the day
started. She told them Fatimah would come to them no
more. That Fatimah was dead. Imaad said nothing but
wrestled his school bag onto his shoulder and strode out
the door. I did not want him to go away from us, and
knew I should have restrained him, but I could not. He
was gone so quickly. He is even now dealing with this
news by sticking to his routine, but soon he will let out
his anger and I will need to be there when he does.

While Imaad shouldered the news like a man beyond
his years, my daughter Aalia burst into tears and rushed
to her mother. They sobbed and sobbed. It was a hard
thing to bear and I found myself weeping just to hear
it. And little Fatimah, though she knew something was

wrong, did not really understand. Her questions told of her struggle to comprehend.

'No more dressing?'

Saleema shook her head.

'No more playing?'

Saleema shook her head again, while my own throat was too full of wet sand to speak.

'No more cooking?'

At this our cook rushed over and wrapped up Fatimah and grabbed Aalia, enfolding them both in an embrace. Though she too was weeping, she declared that today they would all be busy and prepare food just like Fatimah would prepare. Such a wise woman. That is what the girls needed. Imaad needed such a distraction too, but he was long gone.

And so it is this morning. Our cook has started the day early with Aalia and Fatimah, and the three of them are occupied baking pastries. Fatimah is burbling a song we heard our dead Fatimah sing many times, and I can hear Aalia asking questions. Imaad has gone to school by himself again, just as before, not speaking of this tragedy. I do not think he is angry. Just confused. The cook has bustled Saleema out of the kitchen and told her to dress to meet her friend.

When Saleema is ready, I hold her before she steps out the gate. I tell her she is brave and loyal. A true sister to Fatimah, who loved her as her own. She is joined by Rashida, and I watch them walk down the street. I can tell they are talking, heads leaning in towards each other.

Their walk is a sad walk. But it is a bright walk too. They are going dressed in bright colours. It is unusual these days. But they want to honour Fatimah. Rashida wears gold and Saleema is in bright, iridescent blue. I know that under their bright shawls they are sad, but the colour cheers me as I follow them from the roof, heads bent together like the good neighbours they are. But they do not watch the street like I do. They are occupied with each other, not on what is happening around them. They are intent on getting to the morgue at the hospital. It is only three kilometres away but it is a dangerous three kilometres.

I drive to work. The streets are a little clearer and the roadblock is not crowded. I always think that is a good sign. If the roadblock is gridlocked I get nervous. Everybody is nervous. Everybody is frantic. The soldiers are on edge. But not today. My Datsun wobbles down the road, lurches at slow speed through the traffic circle and I squeeze my car alongside lots of other vehicles parked near closed-down shops. Mahrus greets me as I open the shop and we exchange our usual pleasantries. I am startled when people enter the shop as soon as I open. A woman and her teenage son. I have not seen them before and I watch them closely. They ask about material and about prices. He is shy and she is embarrassed.

'You do not have to buy today. You can buy any time,' I tell her. She smiles vaguely and the boy looks at the floor.

'I can't do that. I can't take anything from you until I can pay for it. Thank you. I will pay only when I can.'

I say I understand. 'But I am happy to put anything you like in a special place just for you. You can pay me any time and the shirts will still be here. I want you to have the best.'

She looks at me for the first time from under her head scarf. Her brown skin and black eyes have a haunted look. I read what is on her face. She wants her boy to have the best but she cannot buy it for him. I want to tell her I know her dilemma. 'Here,' I say to the boy, 'go and order some coffee for us all from Mahrus next door.'

After he leaves I turn to his mother. 'I know what you are trying to do. And I know how hard it is. But I want you to know you can put good shirts aside. You can pay me whenever you are able. And you can come in here as often as you need to help him decide what shirts he really likes.'

I imagine that her face softens. It is hard to tell. There is a long pause as she studies me without speaking. Then her boy walks in with the coffees on a silver tray. We drink in silence. She nods her thanks, replaces the tumbler on the tray her boy still holds, and walks out. How sad. Her boy follows her, returning the tray to Mahrus. Yet I am greatly encouraged. Even if she could not buy shirts for her boy she at least took the time to look around.

Mahrus is amused. He raises his coffee tumbler to me as I step out onto the street to join him.

'An early customer. Is that a good sign, my friend? Or was she just trying to impress her boy?'

'It is always a good sign, Mahrus. All these things are good signs. Your coffee is a good sign. It's a good sign that you are still out here on the street selling and that no one has shot you yet.'

He laughs and pours more coffee and offers a small tray of dates. He is always generous.

We sit for some time in the shade. By now we have new canvas awnings over our shopfronts. We are planning to plaster and paint the fronts. It is a big job.

I have an idea.

At the morning break the usual crowd of young men comes for refreshment but really to talk politics with Mahrus. I wait until they have stopped behaving like a flock of starlings and have seated themselves.

'There is a price to pay for liberal politics,' I announce with gravitas. They look at me. I have never spoken about politics with them. Even Mahrus is surprised. 'Ah, yes, a costly price for liberal politics and the freedom to speak its themes without fear of being snitched to the secret police.'

Some of the boys shift in their seats and glance at each other. One speaks from the safety of the back of the group. 'You are right. Every country that speaks freely about politics has paid a price in blood. Revolutionary blood. The blood of defenders. The blood of men who stand up for what is right.'

'Uh-huh, and in the case of Baghdad the price of free discussion is your one day off this Saturday. You are all going to be here after second prayers to help

Mahrus and me plaster up and paint the outside of these shops.'

At that they burst out laughing and slap each other's shoulders, some, I suspect, in relief. They were not sure where my conversation was going. Some sip their coffee and others start to talk with Mahrus about what he needs doing, when two shots across the street stop us short. Everyone crouches down and I back into the doorway of my shop.

Shouting and yelling from the shop owned by the man who sells camping goods and electronics. Another shot. Screaming from a woman. No one moves. We are too much creatures of habit. Up and down the street the few pedestrians have retreated but, like me, they remain partially visible in doorways and behind parked vehicles.

Suddenly three armoured cars appear off the traffic circle and pull up in front of us in a swirl of dust and grinding gravel. Six heavily armed men rush from them into the store and then emerge, dragging out the owner, handcuffed and bleeding from his scalp and his arms. He vanishes into one of the armoured cars with a clang. Following him out of the shop are young men dressed as urchins, tucking handguns into their trousers. They start talking idly to newly arrived police, then start laughing. They turn and look in our direction and at Mahrus who has now walked back out onto the pavement. Slowly they all wander over. I watch them cautiously.

They are sweating heavily and the roughly dressed men are shaking and trembling.

'Coffees for everyone, grandfather,' commands one of the policemen, and our young diplomats shuffle around to make room for the nervous but swaggering men. Mahrus smiles at them and starts to pour his brew, before speaking up.

'This is a man we have as a neighbour for many years. You are wanting to tell us now that he is a criminal? Or is he a different political person to someone else?' Mahrus knows how to go over the line but safely.

The policeman who seems to be in charge growls back, 'A criminal, just a common dirty criminal.'

'Ah, a dirty criminal? Different from a clean one who is able to get away with his crafty political tricks?'

The cocked eye of the policeman is all the warning Mahrus needs. 'Okay, okay. I just want to know how a neighbour of ours, selling small and trivial things, might get the attention of someone like you. There are a lot of you here, after all. And one of him.' He hands the policeman a tumbler and then a tray of honey pastries, forcing the man to holster the weapon that remains in his grip. The tension in the street starts to drift away.

'Not just one but one of many, actually. He is the last. We caught his five colleagues last night. And his boss.'

'But was he doing anything illegal in that shop of his?' Mahrus sounds more perplexed than impertinent. He knows better than most that any amount of criminal activity can happen up and down these lanes. Yet to have a small shop owner warranting a full and coordinated round-up? It is indeed a puzzle.

The policeman shrugs. 'Who knows? He will be taken away to be questioned. But lately we have had a few cells of men rounded up when their activities were exposed to the security forces. Many of those who are giving them up are men who have had enough of the killing and are tired of the lies they have been told. They think they are fighting for a free Iraq or some other nonsense only to discover they are helping criminals. And that only leads to Iraqis dying, not Americans leaving.'

'But this man?'

He shrugs again as he sips and keeps an eye on the street. 'Who knows? Member of a communications link? Supplies parts? Is part of a warning network? He has been mistakenly identified? Or maybe he has been blamed and has nothing to do with anything that really interests us. Retribution for looking at a man's sister the wrong way. Who knows? But we have to pick him up and bring him in.' He sips some more.

'Shots were fired? That means it must be serious.'

'Too many shots are fired too quickly.' He lifts his chin towards the roughly dressed men who have retired to lean on one of their vehicles and talk excitedly while they drink their coffee. 'Those undercover guys shoot at a mouse or a flapping rag. You cannot blame them. Maybe he looked like he was going to run and they had to warn him.' He grins. 'Maybe he was a fast runner and had to be slowed down – he looks like he has had a few scrapes.'

He hands the tumbler back to Mahrus. '*Shukran.*'

With that he shouts to his men, climbs into his armoured car and, with the sound of slamming doors, the growl of engines and crunch of tyres, they are gone, leaving only the hint of diesel smoke hanging in the hot air. Faces up and down the street start to reappear. The young men sit in brooding silence around their little tables. I close the shop and go home. It has proved to be an eventful day. And it is not over yet.

31

Malik

All this time you have been wondering maybe what 'Malik' means. For some it means an angel. Ha, my children do not always think I am an angel. But most people know it means 'king'. How am I both the seller of shirts and a king? I try to be a king in my own heart. I try to be kind to others like I think a king should be. I try to rule what I have with fairness. I want to be a fair judge to my children. And I want to be a good provider for my family. A king provides for his people and makes them safe. You can see I have been thinking too much about being the shirt-seller king. Mahrus laughs at my thinking like this, but it is with humour not derision. He likes it. He thinks if we are all kings to each other we would not try to burn and drown and eat each other. But he tells me to make up my mind. Am I a king or a flower? I laugh and tell him I am both – that I am king and flower – and that he is only a flower.

I arrive home rattled by the events earlier in the day. I keep hoping all will get better. And it does. Look at that policeman arresting the shopkeeper. Maybe as little as a year ago he would have walked in and shot him and asked questions later. I do not think the shopkeeper will have an easy time in prison. But somehow I think he is in better hands now than he would have been in the past. That is a sign of improvement. But I am unsettled by the incident in our street. We are fixing things up and underneath us a fellow trader is trying to unravel us. He looks so much like an ordinary family man who drank our coffee with us. We are all ordinary family men.

I park the car and walk to the open gate. My daughters are playing with the dogs. This afternoon everyone is very wet. The guards, rifles slung over their shoulders, are washing the puppies again. They never learn, I think. They like to play with the puppies too much. They get pleasure from the cycle of washing and rolling in the dirt as much as the puppies do. And that is another heartening thing.

I call the girls inside the gate, ask the guards to let me know when Imaad gets in from school, and close the street out. This is our world and we are safe here. With Saleema away at the hospital I will relieve the cook and prepare the evening meal. There are many hours before we are due to eat, but now is as good a time as any to get it ready. When I am done I climb the stairs. I check the girls. They are sprawled in front of the television watching cartoons. In English. I am surprised how we still have these programs running right through all the fighting. If a family has access to electricity and a television, then their children can still be distracted.

I place some mail on my desk, which is in our very large bedroom, then sit to read a little. I want to start paying closer attention to the ledgers, and pull the books from my bag and place them on the desk. As I do so I am barely conscious of a change in the air. Something tells me a bomb has gone off even though I have not heard or seen anything. I look up. The curtains half covering the glass sway with the barest of movement. It could be the breeze. Then I see the window flex, the light changing on its surface, reflecting a different image then changing as rapidly back again. As it does so I feel the pressure and hear the dull, rolling thump. It vibrates through the building and I shiver in response. The railings outside the window hum.

'That is a big blast. Maybe two or three 122-millimetre shells wired together,' I say to myself. I know from my time in the trenches how big a blast those old Russian shells can make. I am not in a hurry but I think it sounded close. I will take a look from the roof.

I slip back into my sandals and crunch up the marble stairs covered in talc-soft sand that drifts in everywhere at this time of the year, making the climb dangerous. I step out onto the rooftop and into the snapping hot wind that pulls at my face. The trees prevent me from seeing over the suburbs to the south so I turn to my left. Nothing. To my right and I see a dirty smudge of grey being smeared over the blue sky by the wind. It is hard to locate where the explosion was, but I sense it must be within two or three kilometres of me. For a brief moment I worry about Imaad walking home, but realise the bomb has not exploded anywhere near the school. I watch and I think about the people like myself in the suburbs, cooking dinner, getting ready for the evening. Some watching football on television. Others playing with their children. Some still coming back from work, just as I would be doing at this time of the day. How is Mahrus? Is he okay? The bomb was not in the direction of our stores. But killings here are so indiscriminate. A man goes to put his rubbish out. Is shot in the head. For no reason. I keep remembering Ismail. So senseless. I think of Fatimah and of her youth and the promise of her future and the joy that should have come to her. Dead in a random and tiny blast.

Fatimah? I pull back from my musings and pay more attention to the smoke on the horizon. I strain to find the hospital, a medium-sized building lost among many medium-sized buildings. As I peer over the top of the wall I see the distinctive kick of dust and barely perceptible flash that precedes the boiling cloud of dust and smoke that lifts like a small Hiroshima cloud over the suburbs. As it climbs high into the sky and the wind starts to rip the top off the column, my stomach churns and my throat gags. Two bombs. Two big blasts near the hospital. I force myself to be calm. They were in the direction of the hospital. That does not mean it was the hospital itself. But I can scarcely believe the size of the column of black and grey that even as I watch has already streaked wide across the sky, bent by the wind.

One sure way to find out about the bomb is to turn on the news from the BBC or Al Jazeera. I stumble downstairs as the guard shouts from the front door that Imaad is home. Imaad arrives rummaging around in his school bag and pulling drawings out. No doubt he wants to show me something. I will look later. I go to the television, shoo the girls away and turn on the news. It takes some time, but there it is. Reporters standing in the street of blackened cars and shattered shops. I hold my breath. I hear the words but do not hear them. I see the lips moving but do not comprehend.

People have been killed as they lined up at the hospital morgue to identify family and friends dead from previous incidents across the city. People could wait all day in that line, in the dust and heat, and they would be easy targets for these cowards. This is too much, too perverse. Were they there? Or were they already on their way home? The camera stays fixed on a reporter's face. I stay there too. Not wishing it to move lest it reveal something I do not care to see. I lean back and look away from the television to the stairwell just in case, by that very act, I will see Saleema coming up the stairs, pulling her shawl off her black hair and beaming at the children. The stairwell is empty. I look back at the television. There is a new picture. The camera zooms in on the chaotic scene. A policeman waves traffic to stop. At his side is the tangled skeleton of a blackened car. Tendrils of smoke still wisp off its frame. At his feet are what look like bundles of scattered material, stained with blood. At a glance I cannot tell what they are. Some are grey, some are black and others are tan and brown. I look again more closely and see that one is gold and the other is an iridescent blue. The world stops and the screen freezes.

'Baba, hey Baba. Baba? Are you okay?'

I look at my boy standing beside me. I say nothing. Maybe I raise my eyebrows.

'Hey, Baba. You know, I gave that pomegranate to my teacher. He was not there today, but the other day he said he was glad to get it. He told me that he wished every blessing on the family that had given it.' Imaad returns to his drawings. The world closes in.

My name is Malik. I live in Baghdad. I am the flower of this present life.